TAPAS, CARROT CAKE AND A CORPSE

A Charlotte Denver Cozy Mystery

Book 1

Sherri Bryan

CONTENTS

Chapter 1 4

Chapter 2 20

Chapter 3 39

Chapter 4 51

Chapter 5 74

Chapter 6 87

Chapter 7 101

Chapter 8 117

Chapter 9 137

Chapter 10 154

Chapter 11 164

Chapter 12 173

Chapter 13 193

Chapter 14 199

A SELECTION OF RECIPES FROM TAPAS, CARROT CAKE AND A CORPSE 205

A NOTE FROM SHERRI 222

ABOUT SHERRI BRYAN	224
ALL RIGHTS RESERVED	226

Chapter 1

"Morning, Tom!" Charlotte Denver waved and called out to St. Eves' oldest resident as she cycled along the seafront.

"Mornin' Charlotte, and it's a beautiful one, to boot." Centenarian Tom Potts raised his wizened hand and returned the wave, glad of a brief respite from tending to his vast, award-winning hanging baskets, abundant with vivid blooms.

Not wanting to be left out, Tom's West Highland Terrier, Pippin, barked excitedly when he saw Charlotte pass by and ran alongside her, his tail wagging nineteen to the dozen.

Nestled in the South West corner of England, the small, bustling seaside town of St. Eves boasted a beautiful white sand coastline and a 250-berth marina where smart sailing boats, and modest houseboats with permanent, year-round residents, rubbed shoulders with exclusive yachts that pulled into berth for a short stopover, usually on their way to a more up-market destination.

Most of the residents of St. Eves had lived there all their lives with entire generations of families being christened, married and buried in *All Saints*, the ancient stone church that perched on top of the hill overlooking the bay.

For over 200 years, fishing had been the town's main industry. From generation to generation, fathers had taught sons their trade by taking them out on the boats during weekends and school holidays so that, in time, they would be fully equipped to take over—quite literally—at the helm of the family business.

Times were changing, though, and the crisis that had hit the fishing industry over recent years had persuaded a number of would-be fishermen to consider alternative careers.

Case in point, Charlotte's good friend, Nathan Costello, was the town's Detective Chief Inspector. After originally joining the fire service at eighteen, he'd been left with a shattered knee when, on only his fourth shout, the roof of a building had collapsed on top of him and three other men in his crew. He considered himself lucky to have got out with just a shattered knee. Two of his friends had never gone home that day.

Although he'd healed after countless surgeries, months of physiotherapy and regular training to get back to the peak of physical fitness, his injury had precluded him from further active service. On his return to work he'd been offered a desk job but, as he'd never wanted to be stuck in an office, he'd declined the offer and thought long and hard about his career prospects.

His parents had suggested a job with the police but, knowing they conducted rigorous fitness and endurance tests to ascertain a candidate's eligibility, Nathan hadn't been convinced he'd pass muster. Undeterred, he'd paired up with a personal trainer who set him a punishing fitness regime and had been delighted when he passed both tests with higher scores than some of the other recruits. His acceptance into the force was testament to his determination to overcome the odds.

However, as much as he loved his job, he sometimes confided to Charlotte that he yearned for some of the action the larger stations dealt with.

"What I'd give for something like this to happen here," he'd said to Charlotte when they'd met up for breakfast a couple of weeks ago. A national newspaper had run a front page story heralding the success of a neighbouring town's police department infiltrating, and bringing to justice, a major drug trafficking ring.

Charlotte, on the other hand, was quite happy for things to stay as they were in St. Eves. The almost non-existent crime rate was one of the things she loved most about the town. In fact, as a throwback to the past, many of the residents still left their doors open from sunrise to sunset to allow friends and neighbours to pop in during the day for an impromptu chat.

Suffice to say, despite Nathan's hankering for serious crime, Charlotte had absolutely no desire to experience any of the commotion a major incident would bring to St. Eves.

As she approached the marina, the road ahead and behind was clear so she took her feet off the pedals and freewheeled into the turning, legs stretched out in front of her as the bike sped along the tarmac. Coasting along, she breathed in the smell of the sea air mingled with the mouth-watering smell of freshly caught, pan fried fish; a group of fishermen at the end of the jetty was sitting around a camping stove enjoying a well-deserved breakfast.

Whatever the weather, the fishermen took their boats out in the dead of night and were back by dawn to sell their catch to local restaurateurs, and anyone else for whom the thought of fresh fish was enough to lure them from their warm beds at that time of the morning.

Charlotte brought the bike to a halt just alongside them.

"Mornin' Charlotte." They greeted her with fondness, many of them having known her since she was a babe-in-arms.

"Morning, guys. Um, I'm a bit later than usual today—d'you have anything left?" She peered hopefully over her pink-framed sunglasses, into the buckets and crates that had held the morning's catch but, apart from a few fronds of seaweed, they all appeared to be woefully empty.

"Course we do, my lovely! You don't think we'd let you go off empty-handed, do you?" Garrett Walton, the skipper of one of the boats, got up from the crate he'd been sitting on and pulled a large cool box from under the nearby trestle table, atop of which the catch of the day had been so proudly displayed earlier that morning. He opened the lid and tilted the box for Charlotte to look inside. A huge smile spread across her face when she saw four large, speckled sole and six silver whiting in the box.

"Garrett, you're an angel! Thank you! They're going to be fantastic on my specials board. How much do I owe you?"

Garrett dismissed her question with a brief wave. "Don't worry about it. Consider them a thank you for those sandwiches and thermoses of soup you made for us to take out during that storm a couple of weeks back."

Charlotte ran her fingers through her pixie haircut, clasping them at the back of her head. "No. I can't take all this for nothing, Garrett. It's wonder enough that you bring back any fish at all, the state of the waters these days. No, I won't take them unless I pay for them, and that's that." Taking off her sunglasses she stepped back and crossed her arms, head held high, mouth stern, and a look of defiance in her eyes.

Garrett regarded her with amusement. Thirty-five years ago he and his wife, Laura, had taken on the role of godparents to the little girl without hesitation and with unfettered enthusiasm. They'd known Charlotte's parents for decades and, since their death in a tragic accident ten years ago, had treated Charlotte as if she was their own. As she stood in front of him now with her chin stuck stubbornly in the air and her light brown eyes flashing, Garrett thought how much like her mother she was. *Molly had been a feisty one, too,* he recalled.

He scratched his stubbled chin. "Okay, okay. Look, I'll make a deal with you. How about you take the fish, but bring us some more of that homemade soup and bread to take out on the boat on Thursday—there's bad weather forecast again, and we could be out for hours. How's that for an exchange?" He held out his hand.

Charlotte eyed him for a few seconds, weighing up the deal, before grabbing his hand in a firm grip and shaking it in agreement.

"Deal!" *I'll fill four of my largest thermoses with soup and make a selection of sandwiches with a couple of loaves of my granary bread. That should keep them going until they get back on dry land.* She was happy with the arrangement. There was nothing she wouldn't do for Garrett if she could.

Balancing the cool box in the basket on the front of her bike, she swung her leg over the saddle and pedalled off. "Thanks, guys! I'll drop the food round to your place late on Wednesday, Garrett. I'll leave it with Laura if you've already turned in for the night."

He nodded and waved her off. "See you later—take care."

When she reached the other end of the jetty, Charlotte turned left along the marina front, past the bars, the restaurants, the mini-mart and the Chandlery, until she came to Pier

Four, in front of which stood her very own café-bar.

At the end of the marina and occupying a sunny corner plot, *Charlotte's Plaice* had been hers for seven years; so called because after she'd taken the plunge and bought it, the first meal she'd cooked in it had been pan-fried, freshly caught plaice (courtesy of Garrett) with brown shrimp and lime butter.

Originally a mere shell of a building, it had been used for years by the Chandlery as a storeroom but when the shop had been extended, there was no longer any requirement for it. The storeroom had remained empty and rundown until a zealous property developer had seen the potential in transforming it into a marina-front café-bar with a large terrace facing out to the water and the boats.

Charlotte, who at the time, was just about coming to terms with the loss of her parents, had happened to walk past the building just as a 'For Sale' sign was being put in the window.

Instantly, and instinctively, she knew she was going to buy it. She'd been keen to become involved with a project—something she could focus on, get involved with and put her own stamp on—and this little place was it. The money she'd been left in her parents' wills had paid for it and, with Garrett's help, she'd managed to get a substantial sum knocked off the asking price.

Over the years, *Charlotte's Plaice* had become the go-to hangout for locals and tourists alike. Charlotte had worked hard to create a venue that was renowned for its good food, good times and the friendships that were forged there. Year after year holidaymakers would return at the same time, and meet up with friends they'd made there in previous years. It was like one big, happy family, which was one of the reasons Charlotte loved it so much. It gave her back a little of what she'd lost.

Tapas, Carrot Cake and a Corpse

She chained her bike to the railings at the entrance to the pier and pushed open the folding glass doors that extended from one side of the café front to the other. As she slid the key into the lock, she couldn't stop the smile that always found its way to her lips when she stepped over the threshold.

Bathed in weak, morning sunlight, the coolness of the smooth, stone walls painted in the palest shade of buttercream yellow, against the warmth of the terracotta tiled floor, gave the café a cosy feel. Simply-framed seascapes decorated the walls and hung above the maple and limestone bar, which stretched almost the whole length of the side wall.

Bleached pine chairs and bench seats, along with an eclectic array of tables fashioned from driftwood, lent their informality to the tranquil surroundings with soft cushions in muted tones of blue, green and orange contrasting with the pale furniture.

Charlotte pulled the doors closed behind her and carried her box of fish to the opposite end of the café, through a swing door and into the kitchen. In stark contrast to the rest of the café, the spotless stainless steel worktops and bright, white walls gave the room an almost clinical appearance. In fact, the last time a health inspector had called round to carry out a random check on the premises, he'd suggested that if the local hospital was ever short of an operating theatre it could do a lot worse than to perform any urgent procedures on Charlotte's kitchen worktops.

Humming tunelessly, she put the fish on the counter and went back into the bar area to switch on the shiny chrome coffee machine and grind a batch of beans to fill the feeder chute. Considering her chosen line of work, it was unfortunate that the aroma of freshly ground coffee—particularly before breakfast—turned her stomach. She hated coffee with a passion, much preferring a nice cup of tea instead.

However, her customers couldn't get enough of her special blend, so she tolerated her early morning queasiness with good grace.

Switching on the radio to keep her company as she worked, Charlotte scaled and swiftly gutted and cleaned the fish. Seven years ago, if someone had asked her to even touch a fish she'd have run a mile, but since then (and with Garrett's expert guidance) she'd become skilled at cleaning, gutting and filleting any fish that was put in front of her.

The sound of the doors sliding open interrupted her singalong to Dolly Parton's 'Jolene'. She peered through the arch in the wall, which gave her a clear view into the café and bar area from the kitchen, and waved as her assistant, Jess, stepped inside.

"Morning, lovie! I'm back!"

"Welcome back! It's so good to see you!" Charlotte's delight at seeing her friend was reflected in her wide smile.

Jess pushed through the swing door into the kitchen and flung her arms around her friend's neck. "Careful, my hands are covered in fish gunk!" Charlotte laughed, holding her arms in the air. "So, how was the week at your sister's? Did everything go well with the christening? Tell me you took loads of pictures? Great, let's go and have a sit down for half an hour. You can tell me all about it and I can fill you in with what's been going on here."

"Okay. You go and sit outside and I'll make us a nice cup of tea. Or should I say, I'll make *you* a nice cup of tea. I'm having a coffee…mmmm, that smells so good." Jess sniffed the air, inhaling the rich aroma of the freshly ground beans.

Charlotte screwed up her nose and stuck out her tongue. "I wish I could agree with you. You'd think after all these years I'd be used to it by now, wouldn't you? Anyway, yes, I'd love a cup of tea, thanks. I'll just put this fish in the fridge and get cleaned up first."

As she wiped down the counter, she thought how lucky she was to have Jess working with her and cast her mind back to how they'd forged their friendship all those years ago, and the tragedy that had made it even stronger.

Chapter 2

Childhood friends, Charlotte and Jess had lost touch after Charlotte's family emigrated to Spain when a Spanish conglomerate awarded a lucrative, five-year contract to the construction company at which her father worked.

Scott Denver was one of the team of surveyors asked to make the move to Spain, having been offered a generous relocation package as an incentive.

Although the move was only ever supposed to be temporary, the family fell so much in love with Spain that, when the contract ended, they decided to stay. On being offered a permanent job, Charlotte's father extended the rental period on the smart townhouse his firm had provided for them and, in so doing, their new life began in earnest.

Charlotte quickly became bi-lingual, sucking up the language like a sponge, and with her dark hair and light brown eyes, was often mistaken for a local when she was out and about, chattering away in fluent Spanish with her friends.

She was having the time of her life. After leaving university, she was offered a job in a small, friendly law firm as a translator for English-speaking clients. The money wasn't fantastic, but it was enough to enable her to move out of her parents' home and rent a small apartment of her own close to the beach.

Charlotte was moving forward and things were looking up.

Until that day.

On their way to Charlotte's apartment one Saturday morning, her parents' car had veered off the road and into a deep ravine. As a result of the extreme heat there'd been a thunderstorm during the night which, the police confirmed, had made the road dangerously slippery after months of dry weather. They'd told Charlotte it appeared her father had lost control of the car coming out of a bend in the road, too much to be able to correct it.

She'd stumbled through the next few days in a state of confusion. Garrett and Laura had flown out to be with her as soon as they'd heard the news and had stayed for two weeks. When she'd decided that she couldn't face staying in Spain without her parents, she'd made the journey back to England with Garrett and Laura, taking her parents' ashes with her.

Back in St. Eves, she'd moved in with her godparents. She had nowhere else to stay and even if she had, she didn't want to be on her own.

"You can stay with us for as long as you like, love." Laura had given her a big squeeze. "Don't be in a rush to go anywhere until you're ready."

One sunny, Sunday afternoon, Charlotte had taken a deckchair and a book down to the beach. She'd barely been out of the house since her arrival in the town, but it was such a beautiful day she decided to take the plunge and brave the outside world.

Choosing a quiet spot, she'd set up her chair and settled down to a few chapters of Bill Bryson's latest offering when a voice had called out.

"Charlotte? Charlotte, is that you?"

Peering up from under the brim of her baseball cap, she'd seen a young woman with a ponytail of blonde, corkscrew curls standing on the sand a few feet away from her, wearing huge sunglasses that obscured half her face.

Charlotte had been wary. "Who wants to know?"

The woman had taken off her sunglasses to reveal the greenest eyes Charlotte had ever seen. At once, she'd known who the woman was.

"Jess? *Oh, Jess!*"

She'd run to her friend, throwing her arms around her. As they'd embraced, the emotion of the past few months had welled up and over-spilled, the tears running down her cheeks.

"How did you know I was here?"

"I saw Garrett and Laura in town and they told me you were on the beach, but I didn't expect to find you so soon. Oh, Charlotte, I'm so sorry about your mum and dad. I really loved them."

"Yeah, me too. I miss them so much." Her voice trembled momentarily. "Anyway, it's good to see you again. I'm glad you came looking for me."

"How could I not? We're best friends, aren't we? Remember the pinky promise we made when you left?"

The memories came flooding back and, as Charlotte sat on the terrace outside the café, she thought back to when she was nine years old and the evening before she and her family had left for Spain. She and Jess had linked their little fingers and, very seriously, shaken them up and down, reciting the old playground promise to "Make friends, make friends, never, ever break friends."

They'd resumed their friendship that very day on the beach and had fallen straight back into that comfortable easiness that comes with only the closest of friends.

When Charlotte had bought the café, Jess had been her only choice for a reliable and trustworthy second-in-command. She was bubbly, personable and efficient, and the most loyal friend Charlotte could wish for. Together, they made a great team.

She smiled as Jess handed her a mug of steaming tea and thought how happy she was to have her back in the fold. While she'd been away, Garrett and Laura's nephew, Mike, had filled in for her but, as nice as he was, he just didn't have the same rapport with the customers that Jess had.

"So." Jess settled herself in a chair and turned her face to the sun. "D'you want to see the pictures of my gorgeous nephew's christening first or update me on what's been happening here?"

"Oh, no question, absolutely pictures first!"

For the next fifteen minutes, Charlotte ooohed and aaahed over countless pictures of baby Daniel's christening. He really was the most delightful little boy.

"Aaaww, he's such a little cutie, Jess. Y'know, you didn't need to come back today. You could have spent a bit more time with your sister and stayed for the weekend."

Jess shook her head frantically. "No. It was lovely to see the family, but I was ready to come back. It's too quiet where they live, stuck in the middle of nowhere, and you know me—I love the hustle and bustle here and that every day's different. Apart from the christening, the most exciting thing that happened in the village last week was that the church clock stopped. I'm not kidding when I tell you that was the main topic of conversation for two days. Anyway, there are only so many dirty nappies a girl can change before the novelty starts to wear off!"

Charlotte laughed and drained her mug before filling Jess in on what she'd missed while she'd been away. "Well, that's about everything, I think, apart from the ladies' lunch this afternoon."

"Oh, yes. I'd forgotten about that." Jess swatted away a wasp. "Are we all prepared?"

"Yep, everything's pretty much organised. We just need to remember to keep a table free for our three ladies at two o'clock. Actually, there'll be four of them, because they're meeting that new woman here, remember? Y'know, the one who's married to the guy who looks like Jack Nicholson and has the luxury boat on Pier Four? Nice of them to treat her to lunch to welcome her to the community, don't you think? It'll be nice to finally meet her. It's been almost two weeks since they arrived in the marina but I haven't had a chance to say hello yet because the only time I've seen her was when she went speeding past on her bike. She seems to spend most of her time on the boat. Can't say I blame her—if I lived on a boat like theirs, I doubt I'd want to leave it too often either."

Jess nodded. "I know what you mean. How the other half live, eh?"

Charlotte continued. "So, as I was saying, we're pretty much sorted. There's a bottle of pink Champagne already chilling, so all that's left for me to do is peel and de-vein the prawns for the tapas and put a few aside to give the ladies when they arrive. I'm going to give them a couple of sweet chilli prawns and a dish of olives each as an appetiser. They can pick at those with a glass of Champagne while they decide what they're going to have for lunch. Speaking of which, come and see the fish Garrett gave me this morning."

Jess followed her into the kitchen.

"Aren't they fab? I was thinking of serving the sole on the bone as Sole Meuniere, and I've filleted the whiting to bake in paper parcels with olive oil, a little tarragon, capers and cherry tomatoes. What d'you think?"

"Yum, they both sound delicious." Jess smacked her lips in approval.

"Great! That's what I'll do then. Okay, let's get the tables and chairs set up, and then I can start on the tapas."

They carried stacks of chairs and tables out onto the terrace and placed them quickly, before covering the tables with bright blue base cloths and crisp, blue and white checked tablecloths over the top. A vase of yellow silk flowers was set upon each table (Charlotte would have much preferred fresh flowers but they wilted so quickly in the heat) along with a menu, and they were ready for business.

She pulled back the folding glass doors and, immediately, the terrace became a seamless extension of the inside of the café. The doors had cost a fortune but, as far as she was concerned, they'd been worth every penny.

Taking a step back, she appraised the view. As the boats bobbed up and down on the gently rippling water, the sound of the glass and shell wind chimes that hung from so many of them provided a soothing soundtrack for the scenic vista.

This was the perfect spot to sit and people-watch, or simply let the world go by, and not a day went by that Charlotte didn't thank God for bringing her to it. It had been her salvation.

Jess interrupted her thoughts. "Okay, I'd better write up the specials board. You want me to do one for the tapas as well?"

"Yes, please. Can you add sweet chilli prawns, buffalo wing and chickpea stew and tortilla? I made the stew and the tortilla after we'd closed up yesterday afternoon—everyone goes so crazy for the tapas, some days I can't make enough of them."

"Tell me about it." Jess rolled her eyes. "It's because nowhere else around here has them and people love the quirkiness of having little dishes of food with some fresh bread and a glass of wine or a beer. I mean, how many people have said how terrific they are? It was a brilliant idea of yours to put them on the menu."

"Well, you know I wanted to bring something of Spain to the café and, with the great local produce and amazing fresh fish and shellfish right on our doorstep, they're a great fit." Charlotte glanced at the time on her phone. "Right, I'd better go and get started on preparing the prawns, or they'll never get done."

The morning passed in a flurry of customers, old and new. Tom, at 101 years of age, was the first to stop by as he did every morning for his breakfast of two poached eggs with smoked salmon on a toasted English muffin.

He parked his mobility scooter and Pippin took a drink from the water bowl outside the door before jumping onto the seat to have a snooze. Accompanying Tom to the café was good exercise but the little dog always looked forward to a nap when they arrived.

"Thank you, my dear. That was delicious, as always." Tom had cleared his plate and was licking the egg yolk from his knife.

"You're welcome. It's always a pleasure to cook for you," Charlotte called out to him from the kitchen as Jess helped him on with his jacket. "I must say, those hanging baskets of yours are looking terrific. What's your secret?"

"Oh, no secret, Charlotte, just a lot of love and care. Everything flourishes with love and care, don't you think?" He smiled his crooked smile and bid them goodbye before settling himself on his mobility scooter and trundling off up the marina front, Pippin running along behind him.

"I hope I'm still going when I'm Tom's age," Jess remarked as she cleared the table. "He's amazing, isn't he?"

"I assume you must be talking about me?" Jess turned to see another regular, Leo Reeves, together with his friend and verbal sparring partner, Harry Jenkins, stepping into the café. They stopped by every morning for breakfast and their usual 'put the world to rights' discussion regarding the news of the day, during which—as always, at precisely eleven o'clock—they ordered a single tot of rum, which they poured into their second cup of coffee.

"Actually, I was talking about Tom." Jess welcomed them with a smile. "But I promise that when you're 101 and still coming in for breakfast, I'll talk about you just as favourably! Now, will it be the usual two white coffees, or are you going to live dangerously and order something different for the first time in seven years?" A mischievous grin played about her lips.

"Actually, as you ask, we *would* like something different today. We'd like two white coffees and a side order of a little less of your cheek, young lady." Leo reproached her good-humouredly.

Jess enjoyed the banter with the two men. "Coming right up! You sitting outside today? Okay, I'll bring your coffees out to you."

A steady flow of breakfast orders kept Charlotte busy in the kitchen. Whenever she could, she loved to get out and say hello to the customers but, this morning, it had been too busy for her to stop work.

Just after one o'clock, she grabbed the opportunity to take a quick break and went through into the café to sit down for five minutes. She greeted a group of American surfers sitting at the corner table, enjoying a late brunch as they planned the rest of their day, and a young couple who were on their honeymoon and who'd been in for breakfast and lunch every day since they arrived.

She'd just sat down when a young man walked in and hoisted himself onto one of the wooden barstools, a short distance away from where she was taking a break outside the kitchen.

"Hi." She greeted him amiably as she went behind the bar to serve him. "What would you like?"

"Oh, you work here?"

"Yes, it's my café. I'm usually in the kitchen but I'm grabbing a quick break before the lunchtime rush really takes off."

"Do you work here on your own?"

"What? Oh, no, Jess works with me, but she's out on the front terrace. You must have walked past her when you came in."

The man looked out to see Jess talking to an elderly couple in an animated fashion, gesticulating wildly.

"Looks like she's got her hands full." He smiled.

Jess came rushing in. "Sorry about that." She smiled at the man. "I saw you come in but I was in the middle of giving a German couple directions to the tourist information centre. Not easy when I don't speak a word of German and they don't speak a word of English! Anyway, what can I get you?"

"It's okay," said Charlotte, from behind the bar, "I've got this." She turned back to the man. "So, let me guess. I've never seen you around so you've either just moved to the area or you're here on holiday?"

"Neither, actually. I'm just passing through, but I'm hoping to catch up with an old friend who lives around here." The man yawned and stretched his arms above his head. "I'll be staying for a few days, I think, and I'll have a black coffee please."

Charlotte gave him a cursory once-over as she made his coffee. She guessed he was in his mid-thirties, tall and broad-shouldered, his dark-blonde hair and aquamarine eyes perfectly complemented by a light suntan. It occurred to her that if she were ever on the lookout to hire some eye candy to set her customers' hearts fluttering, he would be the perfect candidate.

"There you go." She placed a coffee cup in front of him and took the money he handed her in payment. As she gave him his change, she introduced herself. "I'm Charlotte." She stuck out her hand over the bar and, smiling widely, he shook it firmly.

"Nice to meet you, Charlotte. I'm Blake."

"That's a beautiful piece of jewellery." Charlotte noticed the heavy silver pendant he wore around his neck on a braided leather cord and leaned forward to admire it. "I've never seen anything like it before."

"What, this old thing?" Blake chuckled. "Actually, it's very special to me. I've had it for years and it's never left my neck since I put it on."

Charlotte was about to continue the conversation when she was interrupted by raised voices outside.

The 'Ladies Lunch Club' had arrived.

Chapter 3

"Three of our regular ladies have just arrived for lunch," Charlotte explained. "They're lovely women, but they have a habit of all speaking at once, so it can get quite loud at times." She stuck her fingers in her ears and grinned. "Excuse me for a minute, will you? I must just pop out and say hello to everyone." She pressed a button on the register keypad to lock it and went outside to welcome her guests.

"Afternoon, all. Nice to see you." She went from table to table, spending time talking with every customer, finishing up where Jess was listening intently to the women as they collectively chattered away.

"Hi ladies, Ava, Harriett, Betty, how are you all?"

Charlotte was tremendously fond of the three women, all of whom had known her parents for years, and her since she was born.

Not only had they been incredibly supportive when she'd come back to the UK after the death of her parents but, when she'd opened the café, they had been her first customers, raving about the food and spreading the word far and wide about "the great little place that's opened at the end of the marina."

She knew they'd been largely responsible for the constant stream of customers who had come through the doors during the first couple of months after opening. She knew it, because most of them had told her that "Ava sent me," or "Harriett told me I must come and try your tapas," or "Betty said this is the best food in St. Eves."

She hugged them all before asking Jess if she would check on the young man at the bar when she went inside to fetch the Champagne and tapas appetisers.

At the mention of the young man, all three women leaned sideways to look past Charlotte and into the café.

Ava peered over the top of her glasses and fanned herself dramatically with her napkin. "Phew! Someone call the fire brigade before I burst into flames!"

"Who *is* that?" Harriett asked as she surreptitiously gawped at him around the side of her open menu.

"What's the special today?" Betty was far more interested in deciding what she was having for lunch than ogling the attractive young man at the bar.

Charlotte reeled off the specials. "You'll be pleased to know," she said to Ava and Harriett, "that Blake—that's his name—is going to be around for a few days, so no doubt you'll be seeing him again. He seems like a nice guy."

Jess reappeared with a tray of tapas and a Champagne bucket. "You're right, he does seem like a nice guy… *and* he's single." She raised her eyebrows in Charlotte's direction as she eased the cork from the bottle.

"How do *you* know?" Charlotte's tone was mildly suspicious. She'd become well accustomed to Jess's attempts at matchmaking over the years.

"I asked him, of course. How *else* would I know?" Jess popped the cork and caught the stream of bubbly pink liquid in a Champagne flute.

"Well, I'm far too busy for a relationship. I hardly get any time for myself, let alone a boyfriend." Charlotte's tone was resolute.

"Well, if *you're* not interested, my dear..." Ava dabbed at the corners of her fuchsia-painted mouth with her napkin.

"Will you behave yourself, for goodness' sake! You're a married woman and you're old enough to be his grandmother!" Harriett rebuked her good-naturedly.

"Yes, alright, I don't need reminding about my age, thank you," Ava replied, a little huffily. "There's no harm in a little window shopping, though, is there? What d'you say Betty?"

"Mmmm, what? Oh, the tapas are yummy." Betty munched happily on a chilli prawn.

"I wasn't talking about the appetisers…oh, never mind." Ava tutted and began to peruse the menu.

Charlotte laughed as she went back into the café. Between them, the ladies cultivated a veritable hothouse of local gossip but they all had hearts of gold and she loved them dearly.

Inside, she found Blake chatting away with the surfers. When he saw her, he slid off the barstool and excused himself to the group. "Have a great day, guys." They exchanged casual handshakes before he turned back to Charlotte. "Well, I should get going but no doubt I'll see you around. Good to meet you." He grinned and walked out of the café, nodding to Jess and the ladies before turning left up the marina front, completely unaware of the admiring glances his departing denim-clad behind was receiving.

Before long, Charlotte was working at full-speed again, a stream of orders signalling the onset of the busy lunchtime trade. By the time the last of the specials had been sold and everyone apart from Ava, Harriett, Betty and their guest had left, it was almost half-past five. The café closed at six and she was looking forward to sitting down with a large glass of wine after she'd finished work. Until then, she was curious to meet the newcomer to the neighbourhood, and went out to say hello.

"Ah, Charlotte dear," said Ava as she saw her approach. "Let me introduce you to Samantha Driscoll."

Charlotte held out her hand to the woman who looked to be in her early thirties. Dressed in a figure-hugging, leopard-print catsuit that showcased her vast bosom, her platinum blonde hair was a voluminous cloud around her heart-shaped, perfectly made-up face. Big blue eyes were adorned with spiky, black, false lashes, her Cupid's bow mouth painted with high gloss, baby-pink lipstick. She was attractive in a rather obvious way and Charlotte thought how much prettier she'd look without all the makeup.

"Hello, it's very nice to meet you." Samantha smiled as she shuffled round in her chair and took Charlotte's extended hand.

"Likewise." Charlotte returned the smile.

"The lunch was delicious." Samantha gushed enthusiasm. "Look, I know this is rather short notice but I wonder if you'd be interested in doing the catering for a small party we're throwing on our boat next week? It's *The Lady Samantha* on Pier Four and your tapas would be the perfect finger food. We've been here for a couple of weeks now, and we haven't really met anyone properly. We're thinking of inviting some people from neighbouring boats, along with a few others, just so we can introduce ourselves and get to know people. Do you think that's something you'd be interested in?" She looked hopefully at Charlotte.

"It's *definitely* something I'd be interested in. If we could get together some time, you can tell me exactly what you have in mind and I can give you some costs."

"Perfect." Samantha looked relieved. "How about tomorrow? Perhaps you could come down to the boat after you've finished here for the day and we can discuss things?"

"Actually, the café's closed on Saturdays so I can meet you earlier in the day if that's more convenient?"

"Oh, well in that case, how about you come down at around nine? Or is that too early?"

"No, that's fine. I'll look forward to it."

Samantha pushed on a pair of oversized sunglasses and brushed imaginary crumbs from her thighs. "Well, ladies, I've had the most wonderful afternoon. Thank you so much for your kindness in inviting me to lunch. I hope you'll all come to the party?"

She was in the process of saying her goodbyes when Ava tapped her arm insistently.

"Look, there's the young man I was telling you about."

Samantha turned on her best pout and looked up the marina to see Blake striding towards them.

"Isn't he an absolute dish?" said Ava.

However, far from being struck by Blake, Samantha became positively flustered. "Oh, my goodness! I've suddenly, er, remembered that I, er, have an appointment. I must run." She picked up her handbag and made a swift exit down the footpath at the side of the café as fast as her stiletto-heeled ankle boots would carry her.

"See you tomorrow!" Charlotte called after her before turning back to the rest of the group. "What on earth was all that about? She looked like she'd seen a ghost."

"Well, she was perfectly alright until she saw Blake. He obviously has more of an effect on women than he's aware of," said Harriett.

Blake took off his sunglasses as he reached them. "Hello again. I thought I'd stop by for a quick beer. If you're still open, that is?"

"Of course. We close around six, but you're okay for a beer. I'll bring one out for you. Bottle or draught?"

"Bottle, please and it's okay, I'll come in for it. I prefer to sit at a bar." Blake nodded to the ladies and followed Charlotte inside.

As she cracked the top off the bottle Charlotte asked, casually, "I don't mean to be nosy, but do you know Samantha Driscoll?" She passed the beer to Blake and noted that not a flicker of recognition crossed his face.

"No." He shook his head and took a swig of the ice-cold beer. "Why? Should I?"

"No, not at all. It's just that she was here but, when she saw you coming down the marina, she took off rather quickly. Mind you she did say she'd forgotten about an appointment she had to get to, so I suppose she was flustered because of that."

She chatted with Blake for a while until he left at a little after six. Having said her farewells to Ava, Harriett and Betty, she and Jess brought all the tables and chairs inside before cleaning down the kitchen and bar area. When they were done, they sat and chatted with a glass of wine each. They nattered about their day, things they had to do, Blake, Samantha and, in particular, her strange exit earlier.

"I asked Blake if he knew her and he said he didn't, so I suppose she was in a tizzy because she was late for her appointment," said Charlotte.

"Well, as far as I'm concerned, he can pop in here any time he likes." Jess winked as she topped up their glasses.

They chatted for a while longer before Charlotte locked up and they left for home. As she unchained her bike, she was overwhelmed with a sudden feeling of unease. Something wasn't right—she could feel in her bones—but as she pedalled off up the marina front, a gentle breeze blowing her hair from her face and the last rays of the sun warming her back, all thoughts of impending disaster disappeared.

For now, anyway.

Chapter 4

Shortly before nine the next morning, Charlotte chained her bike to the railings at the entrance to Pier Four, took a notebook and pen out of her basket, and took a slow walk down to *The Lady Samantha*.

She loved mornings on the marina. It was quiet and relatively still, and the sun was gaining strength little by little.

As she reached the boat, she was surprised to see the gangplank down. Samantha had told her that she wouldn't be back from her run until just after nine and that her husband, Gabe, would be at the gym until around half-past. *Guess one of them must have got back early.*

When she reached the boat, she knocked on the metal gangplank. "Hello, it's Charlotte Denver. Permission to come aboard?" There was no answer. Aware that some of the residents in neighbouring boats may still be asleep, she was reluctant to raise her voice too much so she tapped again and called out as loudly as she dare. "Samantha? It's me, Charlotte. Are you there?"

Still no answer.

She decided the best course of action would be to get on the boat. Perhaps whoever was on board was below deck and couldn't hear her. Negotiating the gangplank, she jumped off onto the deck and walked cautiously around to the bow in case, by some remote chance, someone had fallen asleep on one of the sun loungers. They hadn't.

"Hellooo, anyone home?" Still no answer. "Okay, I'm coming down." She called out as she walked down the stairs to the salon area. "I hope you're decent if you're down there!"

She was immediately struck by the opulence of the interior. Mahogany and chrome furniture and deep pile carpets adorned the cabin. Without doubt, it was one of the most luxurious boats she'd ever set foot on. As she moved through the cabin, it occurred to her that something was definitely not right. *Why's the gangplank down if there's no one home?*

She approached what she assumed must be the bedroom and gave a tentative knock on the door. "Hello, Samantha…it's Charlotte. Are you in there? Is *anyone* in there?"

Still no answer.

She opened the door and her notebook and pen fell to the floor as her hand flew to her mouth.

Lying on the bed was Blake. His aquamarine eyes were wide and staring and he was, quite evidently, dead.

She screamed and rushed back up the stairs as fast as she could. With trembling hands, she took her phone from her pocket and dialled Nathan's number.

After four rings, his gruff voice spoke into her ear. "Hello, Nathan Costello."

"Oh, my God, Nathan! You've got to get here now. I'm on the boat and I think Blake's dead and Samantha isn't here and I don't know what to do…"

"Charlotte? Slow down, I can barely understand you. You're babbling. Now slowly, tell me again what's going on."

Charlotte took a deep breath as she attempted to compose herself. "Listen. You have to get down to the marina now. I'm on Pier Four on *The Lady Samantha* and there's a dead body on here. Well, I'm pretty sure he's dead. Can you get here now?"

"On my way." Nathan hung up before she had the chance to say any more.

She made her way back down the gangplank and waited on the pier. She didn't know whether to hang around there or wait in the café, but decided it would be best to stay on the pier. The odd person passed by, nodding "good morning" and she nodded back, thinking how surreal the situation was. Here she was, exchanging pleasantries with total strangers when there was a dead body lying not twenty feet away from them.

Ten minutes later, Nathan arrived with two Detective Sergeants, a Police Constable, a forensic pathologist and two Scene of Crime Officers, or SOCO as they were more commonly known. When she saw him, she remembered that today was his day off too—or supposed to be—and realised that her call had most likely woken him.

His 6'2" frame was dressed in faded jeans, desert boots, and a white tee-shirt that showed off his muscular arms and torso. Charlotte guessed that he'd rolled straight out of bed, jumped in the shower and come straight down. His dark hair was damp and the merest shadow of stubble darkened his chin. *He must have been so keen to get down here, he didn't even have time to shave.* As he approached her she noticed that despite his rude awakening, his hazel eyes were bright and alert. He smiled warmly.

"Morning, Charlotte. Right, where's this body?"

She told him where to find Blake and answered a few of his questions. She told him who the boat belonged to and why she'd been on board. By this time, it was half-past nine and there was still no sign of Samantha, or her husband.

She told Nathan what had happened the previous day, when Samantha had reacted so strangely when she'd seen Blake and that Blake had denied knowing her.

"It seems awfully strange that Blake and Samantha denied knowing each other, but now he's lying dead in the bedroom on her boat, don't you think?"

"I'll do the detective work if you don't mind, thank you, Charlotte." The hint of a smile played at the corners of Nathan's lips. "Okay, we'll need to take a statement from you, and fingerprints too. DS Dillon will come and speak to you in a minute. You didn't move anything, did you? Good." He turned to his assembled team. "Right, until we know more, no one is allowed on this boat unless they've involved with this investigation. Okay?"

As Charlotte gave her statement, she became aware of the crowd of people gathering at the entrance to the pier. Some of them were even walking up towards them, trying to see what was going on.

"Get anyone who doesn't need to be here off the pier, will you?" Nathan instructed PC Milton. "And by that, I mean people who aren't police or who don't have a boat on this pier. And get a cordon set up, please."

At that moment, Samantha appeared. Her face was pink and her breathing rapid as she pushed through the crowd and approached the boat. "Oh Charlotte, I'm sorry I'm so late. I've run all the way. I met a friend on the high street and we got chatting. I didn't realise how much time had flown by until…er, what's going on? Who are those people on my boat?"

"Oh, Samantha. I'm so sorry." Charlotte took her hand. "There's been an accident. Um, perhaps Nathan should speak to you. Nathan, this is Samantha Driscoll, the owner of the boat. Samantha, this is DCI Costello."

"Will someone please tell me what's going on?" Samantha's voice had risen to a panicked screech. "Oh my God! Has something happened to Gabe? Let me get on! I need to see him. Is he alright?"

"It's not your husband, Mrs. Driscoll." Nathan spoke with authority, but his tone was kind. "It's another gentleman." He looked at his notebook. "Someone called Blake, I believe. I'm afraid he's dead."

Charlotte watched as Samantha's face crumpled and she began to cry. Great, body-shaking sobs. *Well, that doesn't seem like the reaction of someone who didn't know the deceased, that's for sure.*

After a few minutes, the weeping subsided. "I'm sorry. You must think I'm crazy." She wiped her eyes and blew her nose. "Blubbing over someone I've never even met. But I feel so terribly sorry for him and so relieved that it's not my husband down there. Why was he on our boat in the first place, do you know? Was it a burglary?"

"Well, that's something you and your husband will have to help us to ascertain," said Nathan. "There doesn't seem to be anything disturbed but you'll know better than us whether or not any valuables have been taken."

"Samantha! *Samantha!* What the bloody hell's going on?" A deep voice shouted up the pier as a tall man with dark, slicked-back hair walked towards them.

It didn't escape Charlotte's attention that he was in remarkably good shape and, when he removed his sunglasses, he revealed piercing light grey eyes that seemed to be lit up from within.

"Oh, Gabe! There's someone on the boat." Samantha clung to him and started sniffling again.

"What? Who? I'll kill 'em. Have they stolen anything? Let me get at 'em." He tried to shove his way past Nathan but he stopped him easily.

"No, Gabe." Samantha tugged at his arm. "He's dead. The man on our boat is dead."

"Dead? What d'you mean, dead? How did he die?"

Nathan briefed him on the situation. "We don't know yet, but the pathologist is examining the body now and SOCO are examining the boat. We're doing all we can to ascertain the cause of death. At the moment, we have no reason to believe there are any suspicious circumstances but, until we've established the facts, I'm afraid you and Mrs. Driscoll will not be allowed back on board. We're treating the boat as a potential crime scene until we know more.

Now if you'll excuse me." He turned to speak to DS Dillon.

Charlotte decided it would be a good idea to open up the café for a while. It would give the Driscolls somewhere to sit while the police carried on with their investigations and they would at least be able to have something to eat and drink if they wanted to. She told Nathan her plan and he agreed it was a good idea.

"That'll help us, too. If you don't mind, we can use it as a base while we're down here for interviews and paperwork. That's good of you, thanks." He smiled briefly before resuming his conversation with his young sergeant.

"Come on." Charlotte took Samantha's arm. "Come down to the café with me and I'll make you both a cup of tea or coffee, and some breakfast, if you like."

She set up a few tables and chairs and cleared a space for Gabe and Samantha to sit,

Samantha shaking as the shock of recent events took its toll.

I know just the thing for that, thought Charlotte and busied herself behind the bar. "Here, sip this. It should make you feel better." She set down a mug of hot tea laced with honey and a drop of brandy and Samantha hugged it between her hands.

"By the way, I'm Charlotte Denver." She held out her hand to Gabe.

"Gabe Driscoll." He pumped her hand up and down. "This is very kind of you, Charlotte, to open the café for us, although I'm sure they won't be too long on the boat. I mean, it's unlikely there's been any foul play, wouldn't you think? It isn't as though St. Eves is a crime hotspot, is it?"

"Oh no." Charlotte was quick to reassure Gabe. "Far from it. In fact, it's one of the reasons I love it so much. I'm sure the poor man simply died of natural causes, although why he was on your boat in the first place remains a mystery to be solved."

She made a white coffee with cream for Gabe and chatted to him as Samantha sipped her tea. He proudly told her that he was a self-made man, amassing his fortune when he'd sold his chain of pet-gyms to a Swedish company for an undisclosed, eight figure sum shortly after his first wife had passed away five years ago.

He told Charlotte that, at fifty-eight, he was well aware of what certain people thought of him and Samantha being together. She was thirty-one and drop-dead-gorgeous and, although they seemed an unlikely couple, they loved each other and didn't care about anyone else's opinion.

He'd met Samantha four years ago at a charity fundraising event for animals in crisis. She'd been waitressing at the dinner and he'd caught her eye following his repeated requests for her to wait on his table. At the end of the evening, they'd left the event together and from that day, had been almost inseparable. Six months later, on what had been the happiest day of his life, they'd married in secret. His children hadn't been invited, though. While he was madly in love with Samantha, they felt very differently about their new stepmother. They were worried about their inheritance, he told Charlotte. He said it would have suited them if he'd remained single until his dying day, shrivelled up and without a woman in his life because then, his fortune would remain unthreatened and uncontested when he died.

As he spoke, Charlotte thought that, despite the age gap, he and Samantha were well-suited. He looked young for his age and had a way about him that was charming and boyish. He also worked hard to maintain his appearance. A devotee of the gym, it was quite apparent that he looked after himself in other ways too. His dark hair was well groomed, his nails immaculately manicured. She noticed, though, that the nails on one hand were rather dirty and not at all in keeping with the rest of his appearance.

"You're wondering how I keep myself looking so young, aren't you?" Gabe's question interrupted her thoughts.

"What, oh…" Charlotte felt her cheeks flush as it dawned on her that she must have been staring at him without realising. "I'm so sorry. I didn't mean to gawp." She looked embarrassed as she admitted, "I was just thinking how good you look together. Despite what anyone else says, I think you look great."

Gabe puffed out his chest. "Well, thank you, that's very nice of you to say. We like to take care of ourselves, don't we, Sammy? I have a facial once a week and a mani-pedi every two weeks. Thanks to Samantha," he gave his wife a squeeze, "I look better now than I did ten years ago. I'm very in touch with my feminine side, aren't I, love?" Amused by his own comment, he threw his head back and roared with laughter.

"Shush, Gabe…please. I don't think it's appropriate to be joking when that poor man is lying dead on our boat." Samantha sniffed and dabbed at her eyes. "I don't know if I'll ever be able to feel safe on there again."

"Course you will." Gabe reassured her. "It's not as though he was murdered, is it? He's just an opportunist who got on our boat after he realised we weren't on board and thought he'd see what he could steal. Before he could get his hands on anything, though, he kicked the bucket. Serves him right, that's what I say." Gabe was completely unsympathetic to Blake's plight. "I'm just annoyed that it's upset you, and about the inconvenience it's caused because we won't be allowed back on until the police have finished poking around."

Then, in a softer voice, he said, "He could have been watching all the boats for a while, you know. Checking for easy pickings.

He probably saw us both leave so he knew the boat would be empty. I obviously didn't tie up the gangplank securely when I left this morning so it must have been easy for him to pull it back down and jump on board. I'm so sorry for that, love. If only I'd taken a bit more care, he would never have got on the boat in the first place and you'd have been spared all this upset."

A knock on the glass doors made them all jump. DS Ben Dillon and DS Fiona Farrell stood outside. "If you're feeling up to it, we need to take a statement from you both if that's okay?"

"Yes, of course." Samantha gave a weak smile.

A second knock on the doors alerted Charlotte to the fact that Ava, Harriett and Betty were outside, peering through the glass. She went outside and, in a hushed voice, quickly explained what had happened.

"Oh no! Not that nice man?! How terrible!" Ava's hands flew to her mouth.

"What a terrible shock it must have been for poor Samantha," said Harriett.

"She won't be having her party now, I suppose?" said Betty.

"Oh look, I think they've come to take the body away." Charlotte hoped the men in the dark blue jackets would be able to remove it soon. The crowd of people gathered at the entrance to the pier had grown and, although she knew it was in the human psyche to have morbid fascinations, she felt uncomfortable with the whole voyeur thing.

"Well, my dear, we must be off," said Ava, checking her watch. "You know how we like to get to the market before the crowds descend and it turns into a rugby scrum. Do keep us up to date with any developments, won't you?"

Despite the news, the death of a stranger—however handsome—wasn't enough of a diversion to deter Ava, Harriett and Betty from their regular Saturday morning shopping expedition to the farmers' market in the town centre.

As they left, Charlotte saw Nathan walking down the pier. His long legs took strides to match and he was standing beside her within seconds. He waited until Ben and Fiona had finished taking the statements before following Charlotte into the café.

"Mr. and Mrs. Driscoll, I wanted to let you know that I've asked if any forensic tests can be carried out as quickly as possible. We're mindful that *The Lady Samantha* is your home and that you'll want to get back to it as quickly as you can. While we can't allow you back on board until we've finished our investigations, if there are any essential items you require from the boat, a member of my team may be able to remove them if you can give us exact instructions as to where they might be found."

Gabe shook his head. "No, there's nothing we need urgently but our passports and some personal documents are in the bedroom safe. I assume they'll be secure until you've finished your investigations?"

Nathan nodded. "Of course. The boat will remain cordoned off until our work is completed and we'll make it quite secure, so don't worry about that."

"Well, if that's the case, we might as well treat ourselves to a nice suite at *The President* and have ourselves a little luxury while we're waiting for all this to blow over. Would that cheer you up, Sammy?"

The President was the only five star hotel in town, situated in a prime location on the seafront.

Samantha nodded, a little mollified. Knowing that a dead body had been on the boat, the thought of going back on board didn't appeal to her at all. The prospect of staying at *The President* was a far more attractive proposition altogether.

Gabe stood up and shook Nathan's hand. "Okay, no time like the present. Come on love, we might as well walk down to the hotel and check-in now." He turned to Nathan. "You'll let us know as soon as possible when we can get back on board?"

"Of course. You've given your statements and your contact details to DS Dillon, haven't you? Okay, good. Well, we'll be in touch soon."

"Right, Princess, we'd better be going." Gabe brought Samantha's hand to his lips and gave it a brief kiss.

As Charlotte opened up the doors for them to leave, Jess turned up flushed from running. "Hi," she puffed. "I just saw the ladies in the high street. They told me what had happened, and that you'd opened the café, so I wondered if you needed a hand?"

"No, it's okay, I haven't opened up for business. I just wanted to give Samantha and Gabe somewhere to wait and the police may use it as a temporary base for a few hours. By the way, you haven't met Gabe have you?"

Charlotte introduced Jess and Gabe to each other.

"Nice to meet you." Jess shook hands before following Charlotte into the café. "Oh, hi Nathan." Like Charlotte, she'd known Nathan for years. "Well, I might as well make myself a coffee as I'm here. They're a cute couple, don't you think?" She frothed the milk for her cappuccino. "Makes a nice change to see some new faces around the place but what's with the fingernails?"

"Yes, I know," said Charlotte. "It's not often that you see a man in St. Eves with a manicure, is it?"

"It's not the manicure that's odd, it's the dirty nails," replied Jess. "Eeeeww. I mean, why go to the bother of having a manicure if you're not going to keep your nails clean?"

"Ah, yes, now you come to mention it, I noticed that earlier. They looked horrible, didn't they?"

Nathan gave them an enquiring glance before opening his notebook and scribbling in it.

"Are you making a note of what I've just said?" Jess asked.

"I am."

"Why?"

"Because every little piece of information is helpful, even if it seems completely insignificant at the time, that's why. Often, it's the smallest details that leave the biggest clues."

He had no idea how true those words would ring over the next few days…

Chapter 5

"Anyway, if you're making coffee, I'll have one too, please, but can you put it in a takeaway cup?" Nathan sat back and stretched out his long legs as he pondered the case.

"So, you think it's natural causes, right?" Jess sipped creamy vanilla bean coffee through a pillow of foam.

"You know I can't tell you anything, Jess." Nathan scolded her with good humour.

"But he's rather young to have just dropped dead, don't you think?" Charlotte was hoping against hope that natural causes were the reason for death, as she was horrified by the idea that there could be a murderer in their midst. However, having seen how full of life Blake had been the previous day, she found it hard to believe that his body had simply succumbed so suddenly.

"Well, even the healthiest of people die, Charlotte." Nathan took a sip from his polystyrene cup and cursed under his breath as he scalded his tongue. "It's just a case of finding out why. And don't forget, we don't know anything about this man. Although he may have *seemed* to be perfectly healthy, he could have been suffering from an underlying condition that caused his death. We won't know that, though, until the results of the post-mortem come back."

His phone rang and he answered it, his response curt. "Okay, I'll be right there." Gathering his belongings, he stood up to leave. "They're moving the body. I'll have to go."

Charlotte shuddered. "Alright, I'll stay open for a while longer if you or the other guys need somewhere to work."

"Thanks, I'll let you know."

"See you later, then," said Charlotte.

"That you will." He grinned and winked before striding back up the pier, leaving a somewhat perplexed Charlotte in his wake.

"What the...? Did you *see* that? Did he just wink at you?" Jess could barely contain herself. "Well, I've been telling you for ages that he's keen on you. Maybe you'll believe me now?" She poked Charlotte repeatedly on the arm.

"Will you please *stop* trying to fix me up with every man that crosses my path? Yesterday it was poor Blake, and today it's Nathan." Charlotte tried to be cross but, despite the circumstances, was secretly delighted that Nathan had shown a little interest in her.

When his work schedule allowed they saw each other socially, but their relationship had always been purely platonic. However, she'd recently admitted to herself that she'd be quite happy if Nathan was more than a friend. Before she'd moved to Spain, they'd never hung around together at school due to their five-year age difference but now she loved his company.

He was a terrific guy—genuine, warm and funny—and she'd been keen on him for months. Apart from as a friend, though, he didn't seem to know she existed. Certainly not as a romantic interest, anyway, so she'd kept her mouth shut. She didn't want to risk ruining their friendship by saying, or doing, anything that would create any tension or awkwardness between them. She had to agree with Jess, though. The wink had been quite encouraging.

"Look, here they come with the body now." Jess interrupted her thoughts.

Charlotte shuddered involuntarily and crossed herself as a stretcher carrying Blake in a body bag passed by. She noticed that some of the assembled crowd were taking pictures and videos on their phones and felt a sudden rush of anger towards them. She'd barely known Blake but she knew he deserved a little more respect than this.

"Honestly, the behaviour of some people is just unbelievable, isn't it?"

"It's human nature. And you're too sensitive," replied Jess. "People don't necessarily want to look at stuff like that, but they can't help themselves—they're just drawn to it. It's morbid curiosity." She drank the last of her coffee and washed up her cup. "Right, I'm off. If you're not opening the café you don't need me for anything, do you, so I'll see you tomorrow. Oh, and Charlotte…make sure lover boy behaves himself, won't you?" She giggled and ducked to avoid the towel that came flying towards her before she escaped out of the door.

Charlotte made herself as busy as she could. There was little for her to do but she had to hang around in case the police wanted to use the café later on. To while away the time, she switched on her phone and, sitting by the doors in the sunshine, opened up the e-reader app and continued with a romance novel she'd started reading the day before, allowing recent events to be pushed to the back of her mind for a few hours as she escaped into her romantic fantasy world.

ooooooo

"Thanks for opening up, Charlotte—it really helped us out. And thanks for feeding and watering us too. You're a lifesaver."

It was almost half-past eight and Nathan had just stationed an officer on the pier outside the boat before he went back to the station. "And I'm sorry it's so late—you've wasted your whole day here. Look, let me give you a lift home? It's the least I can do. You can put your bike in the back of the car."

He didn't have to ask twice. She switched out the lights and locked the doors within minutes. Unchaining her bike from the railings, she walked with Nathan to the car park on the road behind the café. She noticed that he was limping slightly, as he did from time to time when the old injury to his knee was troubling him.

It was a strange feeling but, for the first time ever, she was a little shy to be in his company. She knew it was because of the feelings she had for him, along with the fact that he'd been a little flirtatious earlier on. *Had he meant anything by it, or was he just being friendly?* In her over-sensitive state of mind, it was quite possible that she'd misread his behaviour and imagined a situation that didn't exist anywhere other than in her thoughts.

"What will happen about a funeral for Blake?" she asked.

"Well, we'll do what we can to trace his family—if he has any—and take it from there. In any case, we'll have to wait for the pathologist's report before we can release the body. If foul play *is* suspected, we may have to hold onto it for quite a while." Nathan stifled a yawn.

"I'm sorry. Am I boring you?" Charlotte poked him in the ribs and grinned.

He laughed, flinching away from her. "Sorry. No, it's just that I had a late night yesterday and I wasn't expecting to be up quite so early today." He yawned widely.

"Oh? Why the late night?"

"I was out with Lucy Sanderson. You know, the woman who moved in down the street about a month ago."

Charlotte felt her stomach lurch. She knew she had absolutely no right to, but she felt insanely jealous.

"Oh. Well, I'm sure you must have had a delightful evening." She threw her bike into the boot of the car and slammed the lid shut before stomping round to the front and getting into the passenger seat.

Completely oblivious to her sarcasm, or her anguish, Nathan carried on telling her about his night out with his new neighbour, every one of his words digging a little deeper into her heart.

"Yeah, we had a great night. We went to that new place just outside town—you know, the one where you can have Italian, Indian or

Chinese food and the tables are in a circle all around the dance floor. God, it's been years since I danced like that! I shouldn't really be surprised that I'm so tired."

Charlotte looked at him in amazement. "You *danced*? *You*? But you *hate* dancing. I've *never* seen you dance."

"Well, you weren't around for quite a few years but I wouldn't complain about missing out if I were you! Some people would consider themselves quite lucky never to have seen me dance." Nathan joked as he pulled up outside Charlotte's house. "And actually, I don't *hate* dancing, Charlotte. I've just never been that keen on making an exhibition of myself. I have to admit, though, I thoroughly enjoyed myself last night."

Charlotte could barely trust herself to speak. *No wonder he was limping*. She knew it was ridiculous but she felt as though if she opened her mouth, she'd burst into tears. Instead, she gave him a brief smile and mumbled her thanks as she got out of the car. Nathan got out too and took her bike out of the boot.

"There you go." He set it down on the pavement and waited for her to take it from him. "Charlotte. Charlotte! You need to take it, or it'll fall over when I let go."

"What? Oh, sorry. Thanks, and thanks for the lift home." Charlotte cast her eyes downward as she took hold of the bike.

"You alright? You've gone very quiet."

"Yeah, I'm fine." She rubbed her forehead. "I've just got a bit of a headache, that's all. Anyway, thanks again." She turned and pushed the bike up the path to her front door.

"Don't mention it. And feel better soon, okay?" He called out to her and waved before getting back into his car and driving off.

Charlotte watched until the car disappeared from sight, sighed heavily and opened the front door. Suddenly overcome with tiredness herself, she leaned the bike up against the wall and went straight to bed.

ooooooo

She tossed and turned for an hour and a half before she got up and went down to the kitchen to make a cup of hot milk with maple syrup. She took a couple of chocolate chip cookies from the jar on the counter and sat on a kitchen stool, pondering the events of the day.

She wasn't sure if it was Blake's death, or the thought of Nathan and Lucy Sanderson out on a date that was keeping her awake. *Probably a mixture of the two*, she thought, glumly.

Pulling a notebook and pen from a pile of papers at the end of the counter, she divided a page into two columns. On one side, she wrote *Pros* and on the other, *Cons*.

In the Pros column, she wrote;
I've known him for years
He's kind
He's generous

He's genuine
He makes me laugh
He's gorgeous
He's got a steady job
He's solvent
He's supportive
He's an amazing friend
In the Cons column, she wrote;
He's got a girlfriend
He's an amazing friend

As she sat looking at what she'd written, the word 'friend' jumped at her off the page. The fact that Nathan was such a good friend was *exactly* why she thought they'd be so good together but, conversely, the very fact that he was such a good friend was exactly why she also thought that maybe they *wouldn't* be so good together.

The last thing she wanted to do was risk ruining a beautiful friendship by laying all her cards on the table, only to find out he didn't feel the same way. And the fact that he now had a girlfriend was reason enough to keep her mouth shut and say nothing. Whatever happened, she knew that above everything else, she didn't want to lose Nathan's friendship. That was more important to her than anything.

I suppose that answers my question.

She sighed and closed the notebook. Switching off the light she went back to bed, taking her hot milk and chocolate chip cookies with her.

Chapter 6

The next morning, Charlotte arrived at the café to find that, despite an officer being stationed at the entrance to the pier, a crowd of people had already gathered there, amongst them, reporters with cameramen in tow.

For goodness' sake! She excused her way through them to chain her bike to the railings. *It's not even as though there's anything to see.*

Jess arrived just as Charlotte was opening the doors and she quickly switched on the coffee machine before they set out the tables and chairs. Within minutes, the aroma of freshly ground coffee was wafting out to the assembled crowd and it wasn't long before they followed their noses, ending up on Charlotte's terrace ready for a cup of coffee and some breakfast.

"Works like a charm." Jess grinned at Charlotte as she passed the breakfast orders for six tables into the kitchen.

Charlotte worked swiftly. She had her routine off to a tee and it rarely let her down. In a little over twenty minutes, she'd served up twenty-four breakfasts, all freshly cooked and piping hot.

"Everyone out there is asking about what happened yesterday," said Jess. "I've told them I don't know much about it, but that it's doubtful there'll be much more police activity on the pier today. I'm sure a lot of them will lose interest in hanging around if they think there's nothing to see."

"Good." Charlotte was resolute. "I mean, don't get me wrong, I'm grateful that they've all come in for breakfast but I hate the idea of people hanging around out of sheer morbidness. You'd think they'd have better things to do."

"Well, you know what they say, don't you?" Jess lowered her voice.

"I don't know. What *do* they say?"

"They say that a killer always returns to the scene of the crime. You never know, you could have a murderer sitting out there on the terrace."

Charlotte's eyes widened as she looked outside. "For God's sake, Jess, don't tell me that! You've given me goose bumps!" She shivered. "Anyway, I'm not even thinking of it as a murder. As far as we know, it was natural causes and, until someone tells me otherwise, that's what I'll continue to think. Now will you get out of here with your prophecies of doom and let me get on with stuff!" She laughed as she shooed Jess away before turning her attention to the joint of beef that was roasting in the oven. Her roast beef dinner was extremely popular and Sundays were guaranteed to be busy because of it.

As always, the morning passed quickly.

Leo and Harry came in for their regular chat but, unlike the rest of the week, on Sundays they arrived at precisely midday, just as the lunch service began, and instead of their usual coffees they ordered a bottle of red wine between them to complement the blush-pink slices of tender beef.

At just before two o'clock, Tom arrived for his lunch and settled himself at a table next to Leo and Harry. He loved to chat and a lively discussion was always a safe bet in the company of those two.

Charlotte waved to him from the serving window. "Afternoon, Tom. I'll be about five minutes with your lunch. I'm just serving up a few others first."

"No hurry, dear. I'm waiting for someone to join me today, so take your time." Tom sipped happily on the ginger beer Jess had just brought him.

"Oh yes, and who might that be?" Jess teased. "It's not that Marjorie Wilkins who was admiring your flowerbeds the other day, is it?"

"'Fraid not." Tom laughed his wheezy laugh and took another sip of his drink. "No, it's that chap who owns the boat the body was found on yesterday. Gabe, his name is."

"Oh, have you known him for long?" Jess was surprised. "Just that nobody else met him until yesterday."

"Only since they pulled into harbour," Tom replied. "He walks up and down the seafront every evening and we got chatting when I was out watering the garden. Nice chap. Anyway, since yesterday, his wife hasn't been feeling too good so he's on his own for lunch. I told him I'd be happy for him to join me here."

Right on cue, Gabe walked in. "Good afternoon, ladies, gents." He shook hands with Tom, Leo and Harry and took a seat at the table. "I'll have a glass of red wine and a roast beef lunch, please," he said to Jess. "Have you already ordered yours, Tom? Right, can I have mine with Tom's please? Thanks."

Before long, the conversation between the men turned to the events of the previous day. Gabe told them that he had no idea why the man had singled out their boat to rob.

"I mean, *The Lady Samantha*'s a beautiful boat but it's not as if there aren't bigger and better ones out there. Mind you, I *did* make it easy for him—it seems I didn't tie up the gangplank securely when I left, which meant he could have pulled it down and jumped on board without too much trouble."

As Charlotte worked away in the kitchen she noticed that, compared to how upset Samantha had been, Gabe was remarkably *un*affected by what had happened. In fact, he was behaving as though nothing *had* happened.

Still, I shouldn't judge him, she thought. *I suppose we all deal with stuff in different ways and men generally don't show their feelings as much as women, after all.*

Her musings were interrupted as Jess appeared through the swing door, a troubled expression on her face. "Erm…I think you should know that Lucy Sanderson's outside. She's here for lunch and she's waiting for her boyfriend to join her. I just wanted to mention it because of what you told me this morning."

Charlotte felt her heart sink. As if she didn't feel disappointed enough about Nathan being enamoured with Lucy, the last thing she needed was to have them sitting on her terrace, fawning all over each other while she cooked their lunch.

"Don't worry about it." She forced a smile. "Life goes on."

"I was hoping you'd take it that way," said Jess. "Although, I have to say, I'm a little surprised that Nathan has time for lunch with everything that's going on."

"Well, regardless of how busy he is he's still got to eat, hasn't he?" Charlotte reasoned.

Jess shrugged. "Yeah, I suppose so. Anyway, she's asked for a bottle of Champagne so I don't expect he'll be doing much of anything after they've drunk that." She tumbled ice cubes noisily into a wine cooler.

Charlotte focused on the lunch service, hoping it would stop her from thinking about Nathan and Lucy, feeding each other forkfuls of food as they gazed into each other's eyes and toasting each other with Champagne.

Stop it!

Five minutes later Jess burst through the swing door again, this time wearing a wide smile.

"What are you so happy about?" Charlotte took a tray of roast potatoes from the oven.

"Well, Lucy's boyfriend has just arrived. It's some guy called Philip. Why on *earth* did you think it was Nathan?"

"What are you talking about? Nathan told me that he…that he...um...well, he told me that he'd been out with Lucy, so I assumed they were an item." It occurred to her that Nathan hadn't actually *said* that he and Lucy were together. She'd just assumed it.

"And don't give me that look—you'd have thought exactly the same," she said to Jess, who was shaking her head. "I'm confused, though. If she's already got a boyfriend, why was she out with Nathan in the first place?"

"Well, they were just telling me that Philip's in the police force too. He's recently been transferred from another division and he knows Nathan. Neither he nor Lucy know this area very well, though, so he asked Nathan if he could recommend some good nightlife. Nathan told him about that new place and Philip and Lucy persuaded him to go with them. *That's* why he was out dancing with Lucy the other night. By the way, you've just put nine roast potatoes on that plate. I think that'll be enough." Jess grinned.

"Oh, look at me! I can't concentrate now. Go away and let me get my head together." Unable to hide her delight, Charlotte beamed from ear to ear.

The rest of the day flew by, the afternoon being livened up considerably when Ava, Harriett and Betty turned up and began a sing song which, before long, everyone had joined in with.

At quarter-past six, the last customers left.

"I haven't had such a good time in ages," said Gabe as he shook hands with Charlotte and Jess. "Thanks very much for your hospitality. It's been a fantastic afternoon. I'll definitely be here again next week, and I'll see if I can drag Samantha along too."

He waited for Tom, who was busy kissing all the ladies goodbye, and they left together, singing merrily as they made their way home, Pippin barking enthusiastically in accompaniment.

"D'you know what?" said Charlotte

"What?"

"I rather feel like singing myself!"

If she'd only known what lay in store, she wouldn't have felt quite so cheerful.

ooooooo

It was at precisely ten-past six the next evening that Nathan walked past the café, a grim expression on his face.

"What on earth's the matter?" Charlotte stopped stacking up the tables and chairs as soon as she saw him. Jess had left early to get to a dentist appointment so she was on her own.

"Sorry, I can't stop now." An obviously distracted Nathan continued on his way, through the cordon and up the pier towards *The Lady Samantha*.

Charlotte continued with clearing away the furniture. She usually rushed through it as it was a job she hated doing but keen to still be around when Nathan came back down the pier, she slowed her pace to make sure she was.

An hour later, the tables and chairs had been brought inside and Charlotte was fast running out of jobs to do to while away the time. She was about to lock up when she saw Nathan jump off the boat. As he reached the entrance to the pier he spoke to the officer stationed there before striding across the terrace and poking his head around the door.

"D'you have a minute?"

"Of course I do. Come in. Do you want a coffee, or something?"

"No, nothing thanks. I can't stay for long but I wanted to speak to you before I get back to the station."

Charlotte sat on a barstool and Nathan pulled one over to sit opposite her.

"Right. What I'm going to tell you is confidential. I shouldn't be telling you at all—you know that—but I wanted to warn you. Until the case is solved, just be on your guard when you're here on your own. Okay?"

"Why? What's wrong? You're scaring me, Nathan. Will you just please tell me what's going on?"

"Blake's death wasn't natural causes. The pathologist did a rush job on the post-mortem and found a substantial quantity of muscle relaxant pills mixed with whisky in his stomach. He said they were ingested about half an hour before death."

Charlotte's hand flew to her mouth. "Oh my God, that's awful! So it was suicide?"

Nathan shook his head. "On the surface, it had all the hallmarks of a suicide but the post-mortem also revealed that a large dose of weed killer had been injected into Blake's body. A puncture wound was found on the side of his neck and, according to the pathologist, even without the pills and the whisky, having weed killer injected into his body would have been enough to cause death within a very short space of time."

Charlotte shivered as she processed the information. "I suppose it's not likely that he injected himself?"

Nathan shook his head. "Apparently, the weed killer was injected between 30 minutes to an hour *after* the pills and the whisky entered Blake's stomach, by which time there's no way he'd still have been conscious, let alone have been able to precisely inject a syringe into a vein in his neck."

Charlotte thought again about what Nathan was telling her. "So what you're saying is that…" She could barely bring herself to say the words.

"What I'm saying," Nathan's tone was as sombre as it had ever been, "is that we are no longer treating this as an unfortunate accident, or death by natural causes. This is now a murder investigation."

Chapter 7

Before she went to bed that evening, Charlotte checked three times that the bolts on her doors and windows were securely fastened. The thought that a murderer might be on the loose in St. Eves was a chilling one.

She knew she had to keep the information that Nathan had shared with her to herself but she desperately wanted to tell everyone she knew that there was a murderer in their midst. *They should all be taking the same safety precautions as me*, she thought as she checked the bolt on the front door once more.

They'd find out soon enough, though, because Nathan was making a TV appearance in the morning to confirm that Blake had been murdered, and to appeal for witnesses to contact the station with any information that might help the police with their enquiries.

As she lay in bed, she wondered who on earth could have murdered Blake.

She still wasn't convinced that he and Samantha hadn't known each other although that didn't make her a murderer, of course. In any case, Nathan had told her that the friend Samantha claimed to have met on her run and the receptionist at the gym that Gabe had visited had both confirmed their whereabouts, proving that neither Samantha nor her husband could have been on the boat at the time of Blake's death.

That meant the murderer was either one of the other residents of St. Eves, or a complete stranger. Charlotte couldn't believe that anyone she knew was a killer, so she guessed the perpetrator was someone unknown to her. She certainly hoped so, anyway.

With thoughts of Nathan, Blake and tapas recipes whirling around in her head, she fell into a restless sleep.

ooooooo

"So if you have any information that may help us to find Blake Hamilton's killer, please call our incident room on 070 123 321, where our officers are waiting to take your calls. You don't have to give your name, and we will have no way of identifying you. Of course, if you prefer, you can call in to St. Eves' police station where you can speak to an officer in person. If you have any concerns about giving information, I hope I will allay them by assuring you that all information we receive will be treated in the strictest of confidence.

"Finally, I would also like to reassure the community of St. Eves that we are doing all we can to bring Mr. Hamilton's killer to justice and to remind you that, until now, crime such as this is unheard of here. Although I would ask you to remain vigilant at this time, please remember that this is an isolated incident and we are doing everything in our power to ensure that it remains as such. Thank you."

As Nathan's TV appeal came to an end, Charlotte and Jess grimaced at each other.

"It's a nasty business, that's what it is," said Jess, as she loaded a tray with fizzy drinks and mugs of coffee. "They can't catch whoever did this quick enough for my liking."

"I know what you mean." Charlotte switched off the TV and turned the radio back on. "It took me ages to get to sleep last night and even then, I kept waking up. It's so unsettling."

"I missed the first bit of the appeal—did Nathan say they'd made contact with Blake's family?" said Jess.

Charlotte nodded. "I'm so glad they did. I hated the thought that no one would come for him."

"I wonder how they managed to trace them?" Jess pondered as she took the tray of drinks outside.

Charlotte shrugged and went back into the kitchen. She couldn't say anything to Jess, but Nathan had mentioned the previous evening that his team had identified Blake on Sunday afternoon.

He'd had no identification on him when he was found, but enquiries at every local guest-house and hotel had soon proved fruitful after an eagle-eyed concierge had recognised his description and taken two police officers straight to his room. Inside, they'd found his passport which had told them all they needed to know about who he was and who to contact in an emergency.

Charlotte had remarked to Nathan that she thought it was strange Blake hadn't been carrying a wallet with some ID in it. "Don't *you* think it's strange?"

"Yes, a little," he'd replied, "but what's even stranger is that there was no trace of one in his room either. No money, credit cards, driving licence. Nothing."

"I suppose not all men have a wallet. Maybe *he* didn't."

"Yes, he did." Nathan was in no doubt. "The indentation in the front pocket of his jeans showed that he'd carried a wallet there, and you don't get an imprint like that unless something's made it over a considerable length of time."

As Charlotte sliced tomatoes, she mulled over her conversation with Nathan. *Where could Blake's wallet be?*

As she worked, it suddenly dawned on her that Tom hadn't been in. In all the years she'd had the café, she'd never known Tom to miss his breakfast. Setting down her knife on the chopping board, she called out to Jess. "Have you seen Tom this morning?"

Jess frowned. "D'you know, I haven't. With everything that's going on, it never occurred to me that he hadn't been in today." She and Charlotte stared at each other, neither wanting to say what they were thinking.

Had it been any other customer, they wouldn't have been concerned if they hadn't turned up for breakfast but not every other customer was 101 years old.

"I'm sure he's OK," said Charlotte. "I mean, we would have heard if something had happened to him. Wouldn't we?" She looked at the clock which told her it was half-past twelve. Tom was over three hours late. "I'll call him first." She went into the kitchen for her phone. "And if there's no answer, I'll go round on the bike. It'll only take me a few minutes. Everyone's got their food so they should be okay for a while. You'll be alright on your own for a bit, won't you?" She dialled Tom's home number and willed him to answer. It rang and rang before connecting to the answer phone and she heard Tom's slightly bemused voice in her ear.

"Hello, hello. This is Tom Potts speaking. Can you hear me? I'm not here at the moment but don't hang up. Leave me a message on this wretched contraption and if I can figure out how to work it, I'll call you back. Speak after the bleep and thank you for calling."

Despite her concern, Charlotte smiled to herself as she listened to Tom's message remembering him telling her how much he'd hated speaking into the machine.

"Hi Tom, it's Charlotte. I was just calling to check that everything's okay with you. Um, hope you don't mind, but I'm going to come over for a while. I'll see you very soon. Bye." She swiped the screen of her phone and took off her apron. "Right, I'm going. I'm sure everything's okay, but I couldn't live with myself if I didn't go and it wasn't."

Jess nodded. "Of course. Go on. I'll hold the fort until you get back."

As Charlotte tried to unchain her bike from the railings she realised her hands were shaking so much she couldn't get the key into the padlock.

Please let him be okay, she repeated in her head over and over again. Just as the key slotted into the lock, she heard the familiar whirr of a mobility scooter and turned to see Tom riding up the footpath, Pippin in his wake. He came to a jerky stop and, as she caught his eye, he gave her a gappy grin.

Her relief was palpable. Within seconds she was blinking back tears and the shaking in her hands appeared to have travelled to her legs which, all of a sudden, had become remarkably wobbly.

"Tom! Oh, thank God! I'm so glad to see you!" She rushed to him. "Is everything okay?" Taking his arm, she escorted him into the café.

"Well, apart from the fact that I missed my breakfast this morning because I've been talking to the police for the best part of three hours, yes, everything's fine." Tom was a little cantankerous. He was a creature of habit and hated anything to upset his routine.

"The police?" Jess and Charlotte said in unison. "Why?"

"Because I've been trying to pacify Gabe Driscoll since half-past nine. He's been in a terrible state since the police called at the hotel and carted Samantha off. They wouldn't even let him go with her—told him they wanted to question her on her own, and that they'd drop her back when they'd finished. I had to leave him in the end. He's gone back to the hotel to wait for her."

"Why have they taken Samantha away?" Charlotte asked.

Tom shrugged his shoulders. "No idea. They just said that they wanted to question her down at the station about the murder. Now, can I have a cup of coffee and my usual, please? And can you put a little extra smoked salmon on the muffin? I'm very hungry after waiting so long for my breakfast."

"Coming right up." Charlotte and Jess sprang into action and before long, Tom was tucking into his food.

"I wonder why the police have taken Samantha in for questioning?" Jess said in a low voice. "Maybe they've had some new information?" She paused. "You don't think *she* did it, do you?"

"I doubt it," replied Charlotte. "But then again, who knows? I don't know Samantha or Gabe very well but neither of them strikes me as a cold-blooded killer. Quite honestly, I'm having a hard time believing that *anyone* I know could have murdered someone. It's such a horrible feeling."

Jess nodded. "I know, but seeing as we know most people around here it stands to reason that one of them isn't quite the person we thought they were."

Charlotte felt a shiver go through her and she carried on slicing tomatoes.

ooooooo

Late that afternoon, Nathan dropped in to the café after a visit to *The Lady Samantha*. Apart from the group of surfers sitting out on the terrace finishing their drinks, the café was empty.

"Am I too late for a coffee? I won't keep you long?"

"Charlotte, there's a TV star in our midst." Jess called through to the kitchen. "Shall I see if I can get you his autograph?"

"Ha, ha, very funny." Nathan grinned as he settled himself onto a barstool. "Black coffee please, a strong one."

Charlotte came out of the kitchen, wiping her hands on the towel that was tucked into her apron. It was almost quarter-past six and she was looking forward to closing up and taking the weight off her aching feet. Jess was meeting up with some mutual friends for a drink later and had asked her if she wanted to join them.

"I'm sorry to be such an old maid but all I'm looking forward to doing tonight is sitting in front of the TV and eating pasta," she'd said, dreaming of the bubble bath she was going to run herself as soon as she got home.

However, on seeing Nathan, she suddenly felt remarkably chipper. "You can get off home if you want to, Jess. I'm sure those guys won't be too long finishing their drinks."

"Are you sure? This'll be the second time I'll have left you to lock up on your own recently." Jess frowned.

"Well, you're the only one counting!" Charlotte laughed. "Of course I'm sure. Go on, go and have fun like girls our age are supposed to!"

"Okay then, I will! But I'll bring those empty bottles inside first. I think the guys have just finished."

Right on cue, the surfers got up to leave. "Hey, see you tomorrow," they called out to Jess and Charlotte. "Hey, dude! Good to see you." Cody, the chattiest of the group came inside to shake hands with Nathan, whom he'd met when he and the rest of his friends had been asked if they'd seen anything suspicious around the time of the murder.

"You too." Nathan had the good grace not to correct the young man. He wasn't one to stand on ceremony and quite frankly, unless someone was being a royal pain in his backside, he couldn't care less about titles or pulling rank.

"Anyways, see you around. We're off to, like, see if we can catch us some tubes." Cody referred to the waves that were every surfer's dream.

"See you tomorrow," the girls chorused as he ran to catch up with his friends.

"And on that note," Jess said to Charlotte as she took her jacket from the coat rack, "I'll see *you* tomorrow, too. And I might even see you—dude." She burst out laughing as she walked out of the café. Cody addressing the Detective Chief Inspector as 'dude' was too funny for words.

Nathan laughed too and Charlotte grinned as she walked over to sit with him. She touched his arm lightly and hoisted herself onto a barstool. "So, how are things going with the investigation?"

"Well." He stirred his coffee and gazed thoughtfully into the cup. "There *have* been a couple of developments; one which you may already know about and one which you definitely will not. The first is that Samantha Driscoll was brought in this morning for further questioning. The second is that the reason she was brought in for questioning is because when officers searched Blake's hotel room, they found some blonde hairs that matched the DNA sample Mrs. Driscoll gave us.

"The fact that she'd denied knowing Blake all along makes me very suspicious. I'm not saying she's guilty of murder but she's certainly guilty of lying and, as you know, I don't take kindly to people who lie to me when I'm trying to solve a case."

"Oh my goodness!" Charlotte's brow furrowed as she took in this new information.

"So even though she denied knowing him, there's proof that she was in his hotel room?"

"Exactly."

"So I suppose things aren't looking too good for Samantha?"

"No, they certainly aren't." Nathan emptied his coffee cup. "With an extension, we can keep her in for questioning for up to thirty-six hours and then we'll see where we are. For now though, Samantha Driscoll is the prime suspect in the murder of Blake Hamilton."

Chapter 8

At the police station, Nathan looked through the one-way glass window into the interrogation room where DS Farrell was keeping a close eye on her charge.

Samantha sat at the table, hands clasped in her lap, heels bouncing nervously up and down. She'd waived all her rights to have legal representation during questioning.

"I haven't done anything wrong so I don't need it," she'd told Nathan after he'd explained her rights, but it looked as though she may be regretting that decision now.

He stepped into the room, quietly closing the door behind him. Pulling out a chair, he sat opposite Samantha and leaned forward to push a button to continue recording his questioning.

"Okay, Mrs. Driscoll. I think it's about time you started being truthful with me so, to get the ball rolling, I'm going to be truthful with you.

After locating Mr. Hamilton's hotel, we conducted a thorough search of his room and found some strands of hair that didn't belong to him, nor any of the staff at the hotel. Any idea who they *do* belong to?"

Samantha shook her head but looked decidedly uneasy.

"No? No idea? None at all? Well, I'll tell you, Mrs. Driscoll. They belong to you."

Samantha began to protest. "What are you talking about? They can't possibly be mine. I didn't even know the man so how could you have found my hair in his hotel room? You have absolutely no proof that it's mine." She folded her arms tightly across her ample chest and pursed her lips.

Nathan fixed her with a glare. "Actually, we do have proof. Quite indisputable proof. The hair that was found in Mr. Hamilton's room is a complete match to the DNA sample you gave us." He paused, allowing her time for his words to sink in. "Now, I'll ask you again, what was your relationship to Mr. Hamilton? And before you answer, let me remind you of what you were told earlier; it may harm your defence if you do not mention when questioned, something which you later rely on in court, and anything you do say may be given in evidence."

Despite all efforts to remain indifferent, Samantha's face crumpled and fat tears splashed onto the table. Nathan waited until she had composed herself before asking again, this time in a more benevolent tone. "Mrs. Driscoll. What was your relationship to Blake Hamilton?"

Samantha took a tissue from the box DS Farrell handed her. She dabbed her eyes and blew her nose noisily before speaking in a quavering voice, her eyes downcast. "I'd known him for a few years." She looked at her hands in her lap. ""He just couldn't deal with it when Gabe and I got married. He'd been following us around for months—wherever we went, he found us. So I went to see him to tell him that

Gabe and I are happy now and to ask him to leave us alone. But, I swear, I didn't kill him."

"Why didn't you tell us this before?"

"Because I didn't want to risk Gabe finding out that I'd seen him. He's very possessive, you see, and there would have been trouble."

Nathan regarded Samantha with a wary eye. While her story seemed perfectly plausible, he still wasn't quite ready to let her go home. He had until the following day to prove or disprove what she'd told him and, until then, she could sweat it out at the station for just a little bit longer.

oooooooo

The next morning, Leo and Harry sat in the café debating the circumstances of Blake's demise. The headline in the local newspaper read, '*SUSPECT HELD IN HUNT FOR SAILING BOAT MURDERER*'.

The police hadn't disclosed the suspect's name but the general consensus of opinion was that it was Samantha. No one had seen her since she'd been taken in for questioning the previous day and Gabe appeared to have gone to ground, retreating to the isolation of his hotel room until his wife was released.

"Mark my words, there's always trouble when a new face shows up around here," said Harry. "It must upset the balance of the community."

"I seriously doubt that the young man's death had anything to do with the arrival of Samantha and Gabe," said Leo. "It was just that his time was up."

"Well, there's no smoke without fire." Harry firmly stuck to his guns. "If that woman really is the suspect then she must have done something to make the police think she's guilty. If not, they'd have let her go by now."

"Much as I hate to admit it," said Leo, "I completely agree with you."

The two friends raised their tots of rum and clinked them together before pouring them into their coffees.

"Well at least the police seem to be making some progress." Jess cleared away their breakfast plates. "I just wish we could all get back to living our lives without having to keep looking over our shoulders. It gives me the creeps." To illustrate her point, she shuddered theatrically.

From the kitchen, Charlotte listened to the chat. *She* knew, for sure, that the suspect was Samantha but, in keeping Nathan's confidence, she couldn't share the information with anyone.

She wondered how he was getting on with his questioning and hoped that the next time he called, it would be to tell her that the case was solved, the murderer was behind bars and that peace could finally be restored to St. Eves.

She sighed as she opened the oven door and removed three perfectly—baked loaves of bread. Turning them out onto a cooling rack, she got to work on the brunch orders that Jess had passed through the hole in the wall.

ooooooo

"Chief, I think you'd better come and see Mrs. Driscoll." DS Fiona Farrell's concern was obvious as she poked her head into Nathan's office at just after quarter-past nine.

"Why? What's the problem now?" He rolled his eyes as he contemplated the prospect of going to see Samantha Driscoll again. She had refused to speak to the Custody Officer, instead insisting on directing all her questions and requirements to him.

This would be the second time today that she'd wanted to speak to him. The first had been half an hour ago to tell him that she'd reconsidered her decision not to have legal representation during questioning and that she'd like her solicitor to be present at all further interviews. Unfortunately, as her phone had been taken from her, she couldn't give Nathan his number so she'd suggested that he call Gabe and get the details from him.

Gabe, however, had been one step ahead of the game. He'd already called their solicitor, Vincent Ramone, and put him on an eye-watering retainer to secure his personal services until such time as they were no longer required. Vincent was travelling down from London after he'd accompanied a client to court and would be at the police station by six o'clock that evening, Gabe had told Nathan.

"She's complaining of back pains and I don't think it's a stalling tactic either. She looks like she's in a pretty bad way." Fiona Farrell had been around enough phonies in her time to know that Samantha Driscoll was in genuine pain.

As Nathan approached the holding cells, he heard Samantha before he saw her.

"Owwww, please, *someone!* I need my medication NOW!"

He and Fiona rushed down the corridor to find Samantha hunched over, her palms flat against the wall. Her face was contorted with pain and, as he looked at her, Nathan knew instantly that she needed medical help.

"Get a doctor here, right now!" he called to the Custody Officer. "Mrs. Driscoll, what medication do you need? What's wrong with you?"

"Owww, oww, it's my back. When I get stressed, it goes into spasm and I can't move. Can someone please get my pills from the boat? They're in the bathroom cabinet. Hurry, please!"

Fiona was despatched to fetch the medication, leaving Nathan and the Custody Officer to watch over Samantha. Before long, the doctor arrived and, after asking a few pertinent questions about her condition and medical history, gave her an injection to relieve the pain.

Almost immediately the pain began to subside and, within a couple of minutes, Samantha had managed to straighten up.

"Oh, thank God! I can't thank you enough, Doctor. That injection was even better than my pills. Perhaps I should have you on speed dial?" She was only half-joking.

"We'll tell your husband, of course, that you've received medical treatment here," said Nathan. "Would you like me to call him now?"

"Oh, no. No need to bother him. I'll be seeing him again soon enough, I'm sure." Samantha gave him the benefit of her sweetest smile.

At that moment Fiona appeared, her face flushed from running.

"Where are my pills?" Samantha looked from the detective's one empty hand to the other.

"They're not on the boat, Mrs. Driscoll." Fiona puffed as she tried to catch her breath. "The officer looked where you said they'd be but he was adamant they weren't there. They weren't anywhere on the boat."

"Of *course* they're on the boat! I haven't used any for weeks. He obviously didn't look hard enough." Samantha tossed her platinum hair. "Honestly, ask a man to look for anything... Even when it's right under his nose, he can't see it. When I get back on board, I guarantee I'll find them right away." She took a deep breath. "Anyway, I'm not going to stress myself out again. Gabe will just have to get me another prescription from this nice Doctor— sorry, I didn't catch your name?"

"It's Dr. Talbot." The doctor smiled, amiably.

Samantha continued. "Yes, he'll have to get me a prescription from Dr. Talbot and bring the tablets to me here. You'll be able to give him a prescription, won't you, Doctor?" She looked up at him from under demurely-batted eyelids.

"Yes, er, of course." Dr. Talbot cleared his throat and turned pink. "Under the circumstances I can write you an emergency prescription, even though you're not registered in St. Eves. I'll leave it with the receptionist at the surgery. Just tell your husband to drop in and collect it any time between five and seven this evening. The shot I've given you should keep you comfortable for at least another ten hours."

Nathan interjected. "Please be aware, though, Mrs. Driscoll, you won't be allowed to keep the medication with you in the cell. Just call out if you need it and whoever's on duty will give you a tablet in line with the prescribed dosage on the label."

Samantha opened her mouth as if to protest, but closed it again without a word. Over the past day and a half, she'd come to realise that arguing with Nathan got her nowhere fast.

In any case, she didn't envisage being locked up for much longer. Vincent Ramone would see to that.

When Dr. Talbot was happy that Samantha's condition had improved enough for him to leave, he bid her goodbye and left the cell. Nathan walked with him back up to the station and, as they chatted, he remarked at the speed with which the injection had eased her pain

"It's just a faster-acting version of her tablets." The doctor quoted the immediately-forgettable medical name for the drug. "Although you probably know it better by its more common name."

"Oh, yes? And what's that?" asked Nathan.

"Muscle relaxant," replied Dr. Talbot, cheerfully, as he went on his way.

oooooooo

"Well, that's all the evidence I need to keep Mrs. Driscoll in for further questioning."

Nathan was updating DS Farrell on recent events.

"Don't you think it's unlikely she would have used her own medication to murder Mr. Hamilton, only to then implicate herself when we found out about it, Chief?" asked the young detective.

"Yes, but where *is* her medication? Why wasn't it where she said it would be? Let's face it, if her back hadn't gone into spasm like it did we might never have known that she used muscle relaxants." Nathan's brain was working overtime as he pieced together likely crime scenarios. "She could easily have arranged to meet Mr. Hamilton on the boat that morning after her husband had left, given him a whisky with the pills in it and then injected him, jumped off the boat and left him there to die."

"But why did she tell us to look on the boat if she knew that her medication wasn't there, Chief?"

Nathan sighed and scratched his chin. "To divert suspicion away from her is my guess but I honestly don't know, Fiona."

He stared at the photograph of Blake Hamilton that was pinned to the top of the notice board in the incident room. *We'll find who did this to you Blake. I promise you.*

"Right. We can't question Mrs. Driscoll again until her solicitor gets here so I suggest we pay her husband another visit and see if he can tell us anything more." He smacked his fist against the desk in frustration. "We're missing something, I know we are, and I won't rest until I know what it is."

ooooooo

"I'm not saying anything until my solicitor arrives."

Gabe Driscoll lay on an over-sized sun-lounger on the balcony of his hotel room. Leaning across to the low table beside him, he picked up a frosted glass containing a fluorescent, blue liquid and enough fruit to feed a family of chimpanzees. He raised the glass high and toasted his wife. "To my Samantha, may she be home beside me very soon." He took a large gulp of the liquid and placed the glass back on the table before burping loudly. "Beautiful view, don't you think?"

Nathan looked out across the sapphire sea and shielded his eyes from the sun shining down from the cloudless, cobalt-blue sky. The sand was smooth and blindingly white and, from this vantage point, he could see the marina and the masts of the boats glinting as the sun fell upon them. The surface of the sea dappled in the wake of the canoes and paddle boats that passed by, their occupants having taken to the water before the sun became too hot to bear. He may not agree with Gabe on many things but there was no denying it *was* a beautiful view.

"Okay, Mr. Driscoll, if you'd rather not speak to us until your solicitor arrives that's your prerogative, although I'm a little puzzled as to why you won't tell me if you know where your wife's pills might be," said Nathan. "If we can find them, it'll help your wife and you won't need to go out of your way to call in at the surgery for another prescription. From where I'm standing, it seems like a perfectly harmless question."

"Like I said, I'm not saying anything until my solicitor gets here." Gabe took off his sunglasses and rested them on top of his head. "I know how you police have a knack of distorting the truth. I could tell you that I put my trousers on back to front this morning and before I knew it, I'd be implicated in something or other." His tone was scathing and his grey eyes flashed with anger. "No, I'm not saying a word. Now, if there's nothing else, I'd appreciate it if you'd leave me in peace. I'd like to work on my tan before I see Samantha later on. You'll forgive me if I don't get up to show you out, won't you?" He put his sunglasses back on and proceeded to cover himself in suntan lotion.

"I'm quickly changing my opinion of that man," said Fiona as they got back into Nathan's car. "I thought he was okay when I first met him, but now I'm not so sure. You'd think he'd be at least a *little* upset because his wife's sitting in a cell but, on the contrary, he seems to be having the time of his life."

"Hmmm, I agree." Nathan pulled smoothly into the traffic, his frustration growing at the lack of any new evidence coming to light. "Although he's probably not too worried about her because he's so confident that their solicitor will get her out. We'll see about that…"

ooooooo

At precisely twenty-past six Samantha Driscoll and her solicitor, Vincent Ramone, entered the interview room. He pulled out a chair for Samantha before taking the seat at her side and immediately starting to make notes in a spiral-bound writing pad.

A po-faced legal eagle from the city, Vincent Ramone had a reputation for being hard-nosed and ruthless and his success rate for getting clients off the hook was legendary.

At precisely half-past six, he stood up from the table and tightened the knot in his tie. "I think that just about covers everything, DCI Costello," he said, with the briefest of thin smiles. "As you have not yet charged my client and you have confirmed that you have nothing with which to charge her, she will be accompanying me when I leave the station in a few minutes. Mrs. Driscoll appreciates, as do I, that you may need to question her further should new evidence be brought to light but, in the meantime, she will be staying at *The President Hotel.* As will I."

Nathan hid his disappointment as he shook Vincent Ramone's hand. He'd known that this would be the outcome from the moment the solicitor arrived. Even with all the evidence to suggest that Samantha may have had some involvement in Blake Hamilton's murder, there wasn't enough to charge her with anything. As he watched Samantha leave the room, he resolved to go through every shred of evidence again with a fine-tooth comb. He knew the clues that would solve this case were right under his nose. He just had to see them.

He called through to his assistant. "Amanda, bring me every file on the Hamilton murder, please. Every statement, every interview log, every report—just bring me everything we have. If I have to work all night to get some results, that's what I'm going to do."

Chapter 9

Charlotte spent the evening making a carrot cake for Laura and the soup and sandwiches she'd promised Garrett and his crew.

She'd made the bread at the café that morning and the smell of it baking had brought customers flocking in. Bread baking, bacon cooking and freshly ground coffee were three aromas that were guaranteed to fill an empty café in double-quick time.

Stirring the soup, she tested it for seasoning. Generous chunks of chicken and vegetables bobbed about in the bubbling golden broth, to which she added a handful of Orzo pasta before turning the pan down to simmer.

She cut three loaves into thick slices and spread them with soft butter before filling one with honey-smoked ham and English mustard, one with turkey and cranberry sauce, and one with cheddar cheese and caramelised onion chutney.

If I take this round at about half-eleven, the soup should still be hot when they take the boat out at two. Charlotte quickly calculated that, on the basis her thermos flasks kept food hot for around eight hours, it would still be good when Garrett and the crew got round to eating it.

The storm that had been threatening for days looked very much as though it was going to arrive that night. She hated knowing that Garrett and the crew were out at sea when the weather was rough but there hadn't been a storm yet that they hadn't come home from safely. Still, it didn't stop her worrying.

As the soup simmered, she stretched out and watched some TV making sure she set the alarm on her phone for eleven o'clock in case she fell asleep. When she was happy the pasta was cooked just right, she turned off the heat and ladled the soup into wide-necked thermos flasks which she put into a large thermos bag with the sandwiches.

Taking the carrot cake out of the fridge she was relieved to see that the cream cheese icing had firmed up nicely and it took every ounce of willpower not to stick her finger in it for a taste. Carefully, she lowered the cake into a plastic box and snapped the lid shut.

She was all set. It was only quarter-to eleven but, if she set off now, she'd be at Garrett's just before eleven. A little earlier than she'd planned but it would give her time to have a quick chat with Laura. She didn't see her godmother nearly as much as she'd have liked and she was looking forward to spending some time with her. She made a mental note to make a firm arrangement to meet up for lunch some time.

She arrived at the house, parking her bike behind Laura's car. The side entrance was usually open but since the murder, it had been firmly locked from morning till night. She knocked on the door and Laura opened it within seconds.

"Charlotte! It's so good to see you. Come in, love." Laura enveloped her in a huge hug before pulling her inside. Looking down at the thermos bag, she said, "Thanks so much for making all this food for Garrett and the guys. It's just what they need when there's bad weather about. They can be so exhausted by the time they've taken the boat through it, all they want to do is sit down and have something hot and ready to eat."

"It was my pleasure. Garrett's done enough favours for me over the years—it's the least I can do. Is he asleep?"

"Yeah." Laura looked at her watch. "I'll wake him at twelve. Now come on, come into the living room and sit down with me for a while." She switched off the TV. "You can put your bike in the back of the car and I'll take you home later, okay?"

"Okay, that'd be great, thanks. By the way, there's something in the bag for you too." Charlotte grinned.

Five minutes later they were catching up on each other's news, curled up on the couch with a pot of tea and a generous slice of carrot cake each. After all the stress of the past few days, Charlotte relaxed for the first time since Saturday morning when she'd found Blake's body on the boat.

The time flew by and Charlotte couldn't stop the yawn that crept up on her. "Oh, I'm sorry." She held her hand over her mouth. "I must be more tired than I realised."

"Don't worry about it." Laura squeezed her hand and jumped up from the couch. "I'm just going to wake up Snoring Beauty and then I'll drive you home."

Five minutes later Garrett was running down the stairs, his hair sticking up and his eyes bleary. "I couldn't let you go without saying thank you." He caught Charlotte in a bear hug and kissed the top of her head.

"You take care, okay?" said Charlotte.

"Always do, but when there's a storm brewin', we're all extra careful, so don't you worry about us." He smiled and ruffled her hair.

"Right, come on then, let's get going." Laura picked up her keys.

"I'll see you soon." Charlotte waved to Garrett, not knowing that she'd be seeing him again much sooner than she'd bargained for.

ooooooo

Following another restless night's sleep, Charlotte arrived early at the café the next morning to be approached by a reporter who asked for a comment on the latest development in the murder case.

"What development?" she asked, as she chained her bike to the railings.

"Oh, you haven't heard? Samantha Driscoll was released without charge late yesterday afternoon, which means, of course, that there's still a killer on the loose."

"What?" Charlotte's voice was a high-pitched squeak. "Oh no! Are you sure?"

"Positive. DCI Costello confirmed it last night. Didn't you see it on the late local news bulletin?"

"No, I was busy last night." She wondered why Laura, who was an avid follower of the local news, hadn't mentioned anything about it and then remembered that when the late bulletin had been on, the TV had been off and they'd been chatting over tea and carrot cake.

"So, do you have any comment?" The reporter shoved her tape recorder under Charlotte's nose.

"Only that I'm very disappointed that the main suspect has been released, and that I hope the murderer is caught soon. I'm sure we all feel the same. That's all I have to say."

The reporter scuttled off to the other end of the marina where she'd spied more unsuspecting residents to pounce on.

"Has she gone?" A furtive voice whispered.

Charlotte almost jumped out of her skin. Looking up from her bunch of keys, she saw Nathan poking his head around the side of the café.

"Yes, I think so, but you'd better come inside quick. Those newspaper hacks can sniff out a Detective Chief Inspector a mile away." Charlotte grinned as she whispered back.

Nathan followed her in and pulled the glass doors shut behind him. He took off his jacket and hung it on the back of a chair before making himself comfortable at the bar.

Charlotte was about to ask him about Samantha when his phone rang. He strode around the café as he talked, animatedly and with authority, and Charlotte's eyes never left him as he moved about.

Tapas, Carrot Cake and a Corpse

Having celebrated his 40th birthday the month before, Nathan was in great shape. He ran, cycled and swam at every opportunity and his lean, muscular physique was the result of a strict fitness routine.

The injury he'd sustained during his early days as a fire-fighter had spurred him on to keep his body as strong as possible. Before being discharged from hospital, two doctors had told him his knee was so badly damaged, it was unlikely that he'd ever walk again without a stick. Their prognosis had not only scared the living daylights out of him, it had made him determined to prove them wrong. Many months later he'd walked back into the hospital, unaided, and the doctors had proclaimed him a medical miracle.

That had been a good day.

He finished his call and sat down again. "Sorry about that. Where were we?"

"I was just about to ask you about Samantha. That reporter said she's been released?" Charlotte put his coffee down in front of him.

"Yep, 'fraid so."

"I'm really sorry." Charlotte put her hand over his and gave it a squeeze. "I know how hard you're working to get a result on this case."

"Not as sorry as I am," said Nathan. "Er, can I have my hand back? I need to open this pack of sugar, y'see. Although, I could always use my teeth I suppose."

"What? Oh, I'm sorry. Yes, of course." Charlotte giggled self-consciously as she let go of his hand.

Nathan sighed. "I spent all last night going over the case notes. We're so close to solving this, I just know we are. Trouble is, we're not close enough."

"At least you managed to identify Blake. That was a huge breakthrough," Charlotte said, encouragingly.

"Yeah, but I wish we could give his parents something more. Okay, we've got his passport and his clothes, but I'd love to find that wallet too. Not just because it may help with the investigation, but it would be something really personal of his that we could pass on to them. Us men are very attached to our wallets, y'know."

"What about his pendant?"

"Pendant? What pendant?"

"The silver pendant he wore around his neck. He told me he never took it off—sentimental reasons, I think. He'd had it for years, apparently."

Nathan got out his notebook. "Are you absolutely sure about that?" He scribbled away.

"Well, I'm absolutely sure that's what he told me. I asked him about it because it was so unusual, and that's what he said."

"Well." Nathan snapped his notebook shut. "The pathologist also mentioned that Blake had a thin red mark around the back of his neck. Perhaps the pendant had been pulled off?"

"Well, if it was, it would certainly have left a mark," said Charlotte. "It was on a piece of leather cord and I don't think it would have broken without a pretty hard tug. Maybe someone stole it from him?"

"Hmmm, it's possible but he looked like he could handle himself and, if this pendant was as special to him as he claimed it was, I doubt he would have let someone take it without a fight." Nathan rubbed his chin. "Thing is, there were no signs on his body to suggest that he'd been involved in an altercation so, at this stage, I can only assume, as this pendant *and* his wallet have both mysteriously gone missing, that the murderer took them *after* Blake was dead."

Charlotte patted his arm. "Don't worry. We'll get to the bottom of it soon enough. I'm sure we will."

Nathan grinned and shook his head. "There is no "we" Charlotte. "We" are not working this case, *I* am, so promise me you won't go getting any of your crazy ideas, okay?"

Charlotte nodded, careful not to commit her promise to words. She was so desperate for peace to be restored in St. Eves, she was willing to do anything to help get things back to normal. She'd already decided that if she had a hunch, she was going to act on it. She was fed up of being scared in her own town. In her own home. It was time to start taking the initiative.

Blissfully unaware of her intentions, Nathan finished his coffee. "Right, I'd better be off, but I'll speak to you soon." He picked up his jacket and was about to leave when Garrett came striding across the terrace, carrying a large black bag.

"Hey, Garrett! Long time, no see." Nathan greeted his old friend, grabbing his calloused, fisherman's hand in his own.

"Am I glad to see you." Charlotte breathed a sigh of relief. "The sea was so rough last night you must have had to work really hard to keep the boat under control?"

"It's been worse but, yeah, it was pretty bumpy for a while. I can tell you, once it had calmed down, we were so grateful for that food." Garrett hugged his goddaughter.

"Anyway, I'm glad you're here, Nathan, because it's you I wanted to see. There's something in this bag you might be interested in. Charlotte, there's a lot of sand in here so it's going to make a bit of a mess. Is that okay?"

"Of course. I'll just sweep it up." Charlotte was keen to see what was in the bag for herself.

Garrett took out a large piece of rubber, strung with seaweed and covered in sand, and waited for Nathan's response.

"Very interesting," said Nathan. "What is it?"

"Good grief, man! It's a good thing you never became a fisherman. It's part of an inflatable life boat. We found it drifting close to the shore when we were bringing the boat back in this morning."

"Ah, right." Nathan scratched his head. "I'm sorry, but I'm obviously missing something because I have no idea what I'm supposed to be looking at."

"Here, look at this." Garrett opened up the piece of rubber to its full width and the letters *NTHA* became visible in large white print.

"NTHA?" Nathan's puzzled expression was replaced by one of enlightenment as the penny suddenly dropped. "My God, *The Lady Samantha*!' This is a piece of the life boat from *The Lady Samantha,* isn't it?" His brow furrowed. "Hang on, though. The life boat isn't missing from the boat—we checked that already. Could it be possible there was a second one?"

Garrett scratched his head. "For a boat that size, one is usually sufficient, but yeah, it's possible."

"So, the murderer could have killed Blake before escaping on the spare life boat…" Nathan's mind was racing. "Right, I'm taking this down to the station. I'm not sure that forensics will be able to get much from it after all the time it's been in the water, but I know they'll have a damn good try. Thanks for bringing this to me, Garrett. If you hadn't found it, we would never even have considered the possibility of a second life boat."

"But," said Charlotte, "the fact that you found it all torn up and floating in the sea doesn't bode well for whoever was on it, does it? I mean, maybe they went into the rocks—you know how treacherous they can be—and got ripped to pieces." She shivered at the thought.

"No. This material hasn't been shredded by the waves or the rocks," said Garrett. "Look, it's been cut with a knife—a jagged fisherman's knife like this." He took his knife from the pocket of his jacket and showed it to Nathan.

"So, the last person to use this life boat deliberately destroyed it afterwards?"

"Looks that way," said Garrett. "And that's not all." He took something out of his other pocket and handed it to Nathan. "This was caught up with it, bunched up inside a lump of seaweed."

It was battered almost beyond recognition, misshapen and soaked with seawater, but there was no doubt that what Nathan was holding in his hand was Blake Hamilton's missing wallet.

Chapter 10

"Well, there was still money in the wallet," said Nathan, "and his driving licence and all his credit cards, so whoever killed him wasn't interested in robbing him."

"What about fingerprints?"

"No, no fingerprints at all. There *was* something in the front compartment though. It looks like it may have been a business card but it was so wet, there's no way of knowing for sure because it had turned to mush. All forensics could make out was something blue and green in the top right-hand corner. Otherwise, there was nothing. Absolutely zilch."

"That's weird. Why take someone's wallet from them but leave the money in it? I don't get it."

"Search me," said Nathan. "Look, I've got a briefing to get to. I'll catch up with you later, okay? Bye."

Tapas, Carrot Cake and a Corpse

Charlotte pressed the 'End Call' button on her phone and locked the doors to the café. All day long, she'd been distracted by Garrett's visit and the questions it had raised. Not for the first time, she wished she could have spoken to Jess about things but knew she couldn't.

As hard as she tried to put the fact that there was still a killer on the loose to the back of her mind, it had proved rather difficult that day as Ava, Harriett and Betty had spent the entire afternoon at the café debating the murder at length with Leo and Harry. They'd seen Samantha and Gabe in the town that morning, surrounded by reporters, and had rushed back to tell Charlotte that the couple had said to expect them for lunch on Sunday at two o'clock.

"And Gabe asked if you could chill a couple of cases of pink Champagne," Ava had said.

"Yes, evidently, they're going to celebrate Samantha's release in style," Harriett had reported, excitedly, "and we're all invited."

"Oooh, if the Champagne's going to be flowing, I think we'd better have our lunch early." Betty had suggested. "What d'you say, ladies?"

"Suits us," Ava and Harriett had replied in unison.

"Right, you'd better put us down for three roast beef lunches at twelve-thirty." Betty could hardly conceal her excitement. "Oh, I do love a party!"

As Charlotte cycled up the marina front, she saw Cody and his friends sitting in *The Bottle of Beer*, a music bar popular with other surfers and which, as the name suggested, only served bottles of beer. They waved when they saw her and she stopped the bike outside the bar.

"Hi guys. How was the surf today?"

"Fantastic! We, like, caught the tail end of last night's storm and the waves have been, like, freakin' awesome." As was usually the case, Cody did all the talking, the others happy to just sit back, spectate and drink their beers.

He was explaining a complicated surfing technique to Charlotte in some detail, when she saw something that made the hairs on the back of her neck stand up. Around Cody's neck, on a silver chain, was a pendant exactly like the one Blake had worn. It wasn't on a leather cord, but it looked exactly the same.

Surely Cody can't be the killer?

She cast her mind back to the day she'd met Blake. Cody and his friends had been in the café that day, and Blake had spent some time chatting with them.

Perhaps Cody had taken a liking to the pendant, followed him onto The Lady Samantha the following day, murdered him and then snatched it for himself?

A thousand thoughts were racing through her mind as she reasoned with herself, trying to look interested in what Cody was telling her.

No, that's just too far-fetched to be true. And anyway, I can't imagine Cody putting time aside on his holiday to buy weed killer, let alone get hold of muscle relaxants and a syringe. No, it can't be him. I'm just going to ask him where he got the pendant from—there's bound to be a perfectly reasonable explanation. If he is guilty of anything, there are enough people around that he's not going to do anything to me here. I can always call Nathan if I feel threatened.

"So, yeah, there was like, this much air between like, the board and the wave." Cody spread his hands wide apart. "Freakin' awesome!" he repeated, and held out his hand for Charlotte to high-five him.

"Oh, yeah, er, awesome," she said, distractedly smacking her hand against his. "Um, Cody, that pendant you're wearing. Where did you get it?"

"Huh? Oh this. I found it on the beach this morning. Reckon it was washed up during the storm. It had a piece of leather tied to it, but that was, like, broken, so I just put it on my chain. Cool, huh?"

In an instant, Charlotte's heart rate slowed as all her concerns disappeared. Unless he was an amazing actor, there was no way that Cody was the murderer.

He's not a killer. I just know it.

"Look, Cody. I think that pendant may have belonged to Blake. You know, the man who was found on *The Lady Samantha* last week. And I think the police are going to need it as evidence. Who knows, if it turns out *not* to be his, they may even let you have it back…finders, keepers, and all that."

Cody listened intently to what Charlotte was telling him, all the time, his fingers stroking the pendant proprietorially. When she'd finished speaking, he simply shrugged his shoulders and took the pendant off his chain.

"Bummer," he said. "Like, I had no clue this belonged to a dead dude. Man, it makes me go, like, cold." He frowned as he handed Charlotte the pendant.

"You want *me* to give it to the police?"

"Yeah, d'you mind? We've only got, like, two days of our vacation left and I don't want to spend it in some stuffy police station. If they need to, like, speak to me, then yeah, I'll go and see them, but if they don't …" He trailed off.

"Okay, I'll give this to DCI Costello and if he needs to speak to you, he'll let you know." Charlotte squeezed the young man's arm and he blushed scarlet. "Thanks, Cody. This could really help the investigation."

"Hey, like, no worries…s'the least I could do."

"Right, I'm off. I'll see you some time." Charlotte hoisted herself back on her saddle and cycled off.

As soon as she got round the corner she called Nathan but went straight through to his answering service. *He must still be in his briefing.* A shrill beep signalled for her to leave a message. "Hi, it's me. Listen, I was on my way home when I ran into Cody. You know, the American surfer guy. I'm pretty sure he's got nothing to do with the murder but he was wearing Blake's pendant around his neck. He said he found it washed up on the beach this morning. I told him that I thought it might be Blake's, and could be evidence, and he gave it to me. He's only got two days of his holiday left so he asked if I'd pass it on to you. He's quite willing to come down to the station if you need to speak to him, which I suppose you will, but in the meantime I wanted to let you know that I'll hold onto the pendant until I see you. Unless you want me to bring it down to the station? Either way, just let me know. Speak to you soon."

At home, she kicked off her shoes and put the kettle on. She took the pendant out of her pocket and grabbed a piece of kitchen paper to wrap it in. Like the wallet, it was unlikely that there'd be any trace of fingerprints on it after being tossed around in the sea but, as she wrapped it carefully, she was hopeful it might yield some clues.

She was remembering how good it had looked around Blake's neck when it slipped out of her hand and fell to the floor.

"Damn it!" On first glance, the pendant appeared to have broken in two. However, on closer inspection, she realised it was hinged and the impact had opened it.

As she bent to pick it up, her breath caught in her throat. "Oh wow!" She peered closely at the pendant, the inside of which held a small photograph.

For the second time in less than an hour, the hairs on the back of her neck stood on end and she jumped as her phone rang loudly.

"Hi. I just got your message. Look, it's not that I'm not grateful for the information, but how many times do I have to tell you not to get involved in police business? You should have called me straight away and I'd have come down to speak to Cody. You don't *know* he's not the killer—not for sure—and I'd never forgive myself if anything happened to you. Anyway, I'm sending DS Dillon down to speak to him now, and I'll come round and get that pendant if you're going to be home for a while?" Nathan's deep voice was reassuring in her ear. "Charlotte? You there?"

"Nathan, you need to get here right away. You are not going to *believe* what I'm looking at!"

CHAPTER 11

Charlotte lay awake, her head spinning with everything that had happened over the past few days.

The emergence of the life boat, the wallet and the pendant had shed new light on the investigation, that was for sure, but now she was more confused than ever as to who the killer could be. In any case, even if it was Samantha, Nathan still didn't have enough evidence to charge her.

As she tossed and turned, she thought back to the day she'd found Blake's body and, suddenly, something Nathan had said came into her mind, as clear as day.

"Often, it's the smallest details that leave the biggest clues."

With a gasp, she sat bolt upright. "I'm brilliant!" she said out loud, as she jumped out of bed. She ran to the bathroom and pulled on her clothes from the night before and then ran downstairs and rummaged through the cupboard under the kitchen sink, vowing for the umpteenth time to clear it out when she had time.

Five minutes later she was cycling carefully off into the pitch-black night, thankful to have found the torch she'd been looking for.

At a little after one o'clock, she arrived at Tom's cottage. Leaning her bike up against the wall, she crept into the front garden as quietly as she could, praying that Pippin wouldn't start barking. Looking around, she spied a large, empty terracotta plant pot and, with huge effort, carried it over to stand, upturned, under Tom's largest hanging basket.

I'm sorry Tom, but duty calls.

She put her hand into the basket taking care not to damage the plant, its wonderfully-fat buds on the verge of bursting open to reveal their glorious flora. As she felt around in the soil, she found nothing except a couple of wood lice who were probably most aggrieved at being disturbed at that hour of the morning.

Undeterred, she moved the flowerpot to stand under the next basket. "Good grief, this thing weighs a ton!" she puffed under her breath.

Standing carefully on the upturned pot, she delved into the basket and began to feel around in the cool earth. She was just about to move on to the next basket when her fingers touched a hard object. Pulling gently until it was out of the soil, she looked at it in the dim glow of the torch and saw that it was a plastic food bag, its contents obscured by soil deposits. She shook it and the soil fell away. *Bingo!* She could barely contain her excitement when she saw what was inside. She carried the plant pot back to where she'd found it and, putting the bag carefully into the basket on her bike, cycled off as fast as her legs would pedal.

As soon as she got home, she called Nathan. For a split-second, she wondered whether to wait until the morning before deciding that this was far too important to leave until then. He answered the phone after two rings.

"Yes, Charlotte?"

Although his voice was stern, she could tell that he was smiling as he spoke. He was obviously becoming accustomed to her late night calls. "Hi, did I wake you?"

"No, you didn't. I was going over some paperwork. What's up?"

"Um…look, I know you told me to mind my own business, but you're going to be *really* pleased with me this time. I've just found some evidence that I'm pretty sure will prove who the killer is. Can I come over?"

"Charlotte, please tell me that you haven't been out in the middle of the night looking for clues?" She could tell from Nathan's voice that he definitely was *not* smiling now.

"Oh, don't be such a grump. I didn't have time to think, I just went. Anyway I'm back now, and I'm safe, so there's nothing to worry about. So," she persisted, "can I come over?"

She heard Nathan's heavy sigh. "No, you can't. I'll come over to you. I don't want you cycling anywhere at this time of night again. Give me five minutes."

She put down the phone and waited impatiently. She couldn't wait to show Nathan what she'd found.

True to his word, Nathan was on her doorstep five minutes later. "So, what's so urgent that you're riding round the neighbourhood in the dead of night?"

"Come in, come into the kitchen." Charlotte grabbed his sleeve and pulled him inside. "Look!" She passed the bag to him and held her breath as he looked inside.

"Oh, my God! Charlotte, where did you get this?"

She quickly filled him in on her late night revelation and how it had led her to the clues he now held in his hand.

"Actually, it's because of *you* that I found it. If I hadn't remembered what you'd said about the smallest details leaving the biggest clues, it would never have occurred to me to go looking for it. It should be quite useful as evidence, don't you think?" She crossed her fingers behind her back.

"Useful? Charlotte, if this is what I think it is, it'll be covered in fingerprints. I'm taking it down to the station right away."

"So, will this prove who the murderer is, once and for all?" Charlotte kept her fingers crossed. It was high time that things got back to normal in St. Eves.

"Well, it's pretty incriminating evidence so, yes, I'd say so." Nathan strode towards the front door. As he opened it, he turned back. "And Charlotte."

"Yes?"

"Thanks."

ooooooo

All day on Friday, Charlotte was like a cat on hot bricks. Every time her phone rang she jumped at it, hoping it was Nathan with some news, but she heard nothing from him. By two o'clock she couldn't bear it any longer so she called and left him a message but he didn't get back to her.

"Are you sure you're okay?" Jess had asked, after the sound of Charlotte's phone ringing for the fifth time had sent her friend into an almost frenzied state.

"Yes, yes, I'm fine. Well, actually, I'm not, but I can't say why. I'm sorry, Jess. I hate it when people say there's something wrong but then won't tell you what it is, but I really can't. I wish I could, but I can't. I hope I'll be able to tell you everything soon, though."

"You're not ill, are you?" Jess had asked, anxiously. "If you are, you have to tell me, because you can't go through it alone. *Are* you ill?"

"Oh, Jess, no, it's nothing like that but thank you." Charlotte had given her a hug. "It's nothing to worry about. It's just me getting myself into a state. Just try not to pay attention to me and I'll try to calm down a bit."

"Well, as long as you're okay, then it's all good." Jess had beamed. "I can wait until you're ready to tell me whatever it is. Now, where's that BLT and chicken and avocado salad for table six?"

oooooooo

Charlotte didn't hear from Nathan until almost midnight on Saturday when he called round just as she was getting ready for bed.

Standing on the front step, his face was totally impassive so she had no idea whether he had good or bad news.

"Well?"

"I've just had the results back."

"Nathan, for goodness' sake, don't make me wait! What did they say?!" Charlotte could barely contain herself.

His face broke into a broad grin. "There were fingerprints all over that evidence you found. Just one set of prints, so we're in no doubt now as to the killer's identity. It's almost over, Charlotte. We're charging the killer tomorrow." He punched the air triumphantly.

"Oh, that's fantastic!" Charlotte grabbed his hands. "Is it who I thought it was?"

He nodded. "It is."

"Listen. You know that Gabe's having a 'release celebration' for Samantha at the café tomorrow, don't you?" said Charlotte. "They've invited quite a few people, so everyone will be together, all in the same place. I'm only mentioning it because I thought it'd make it easier if you know where the killer's going to be when you come looking."

Nathan rubbed his chin. "You know, that's not a bad idea. I tell you what, this is what I'm going to do …"

CHAPTER 12

Charlotte looked up the pier. The police cordon was still in place around *The Lady Samantha* and a police officer was still permanently stationed at the entrance to the pier. She hoped that, after today, it wouldn't be long before both the cordon and the officer would be removed and St. Eves could resume its usual state of calm.

"Have you got room in the kitchen fridge to put some of this Champagne?" asked Jess. "The bar fridge is just about full to bursting."

"I'm sure there's room. Here, give me those bottles and I'll fit them in somewhere." Charlotte was trying to wedge the Champagne between the lemon meringue pie and a tray of avocados when she heard Gabe Driscoll's voice.

"Good morning, love," he said to Jess. "Is Charlotte around?"

"Hang on a minute." Charlotte called out from the kitchen. "I'm just putting the last of your Champagne in the fridge." She popped her head up over the swing door. "Hi, you're a bit early, aren't you?"

"I wanted to pop in and make sure everything will be ready when we arrive later. There'll be eleven of us for lunch and people joining us throughout the afternoon for drinks. Now, I understand that Ava, Harriett and Betty have already booked their lunch for half-past twelve? Well, I've just seen them and told them I was hoping we could all sit down for lunch together at two o'clock and they said that's okay with them. I assume you can accommodate all eleven of us at two o'clock?"

Charlotte came through the swing door and took the reservations diary from under the bar. "Yes, that's no problem. We'll push some tables together and reserve them for you. I'm glad you came in and told us. We didn't realise you'd invited so many for lunch and I would have hated not to have had enough space for you all."

"That's great. And the Champagne is chilling, you say?"

"Yes, everything's under control. All you need to do is turn up with your guests and enjoy yourselves." Jess smiled,

"Excellent! Well, I'll be on my way. We'll see you later. Oh, and one more thing—everything's on me today, okay? I don't want any of my guests paying for anything." With that, Gabe sauntered off along the marina front, whistling softly to himself.

"Y'know, I'm really looking forward to this party," said Jess. "I know I'll be working, but it's about time we had something else to focus on around here apart from that flippin' murder. It'll be nice for everyone to have something different to talk about tomorrow."

You have no idea, thought Charlotte, as she nodded and smiled.

ooooooo

"We're going to run out of Champagne at the rate that lot are guzzling it." Jess came through to the kitchen for another two bottles. "That solicitor guy is knocking it back like water! Mind you, everyone's having a whale of a time and, I've got to say, it's true what they say about atmospheres being contagious!" She grinned widely before disappearing with the Champagne, to a round of applause from the waiting diners.

Charlotte heard the corks pop, and the cheers that followed, and was glad she was in the kitchen. She wouldn't have felt comfortable sharing in the celebrations knowing what was about to happen.

At half-past four, she heard Nathan speaking to DS Farrell as they walked along the footpath at the side of the café and, despite the heat of the day, she went cold.

Oh my. Here we go. She went out to watch the proceedings from the bar.

Tapas, Carrot Cake and a Corpse

"Ah, DCI Costello, DS Farrell. Can I offer you some Champagne?" Gabe raised the bottle as Nathan and Fiona walked around the corner and onto the terrace.

"No, thank you. We're on duty," replied Nathan. "In fact, as sorry as I am to break up your party, I have a few more questions. I don't mind telling you, this case had me stumped for a while but, thanks to the help of certain members of the community and the dedicated work of the investigating team, I'm delighted to report that I am now able to reveal the name of Blake's Hamilton's killer."

A ripple of applause went around the table and Ava, Harriett and Betty raised their glasses to Nathan and Fiona with calls of, "Oh, well done!" "Congratulations," and "Bravo, bravo."

The look of contempt on Gabe's face was palpable. "For crying out loud! You really are the most inept detective I've ever met. Can't you just give her a break? I mean, you had her in custody for almost two days and couldn't charge her with anything. And d'you know why? Because. She. Didn't. Do. Anything. That's why." Clearly furious, Gabe spat out the words and put his arm around Samantha's shoulders.

"Yes, I'm fully aware of that," said Nathan. "But it's not your wife I'm here to question, Mr. Driscoll. It's you."

The excited chatter around the table stopped immediately and Gabe's glass of Champagne came to a halt halfway to his mouth. "Me?" He was incredulous. "Why? I haven't done anything. Why on earth do you want to question me?"

"Well, before I get to that, let me tell you how we arrived at where we are now. Do you mind if I pull up a chair?" Nathan put down a box he was carrying before dragging a chair from another table and settling himself next to Samantha. He opened his mouth as if to speak, but then paused and pointed to a bottle of sparkling water on the table. "Would you mind if

I had a glass of water, please? I've got a very dry throat all of a sudden."

"No, not at all." Samantha passed him a glass.

"DS Farrell, would you like some?" Nathan turned to his colleague, who shook her head.

"*For God's sake!* Can we *please* get on with it!" Gabe roared and slammed his hand down on the table, his grey eyes glinting dangerously.

Nathan took a sip from his glass. "That's quite a temper you have there, Mr. Driscoll. I suggest you calm it down." His voice was icy as his eyes locked on Gabe's.

Gabe looked down at his hands, red-faced and breathing deeply.

"I would advise you to say nothing, Mr. Driscoll. I would 'vise it very, um, strongly indeed." An extremely tipsy Vincent Ramone pointed to no one in particular and hiccupped. Having been given an unexpected afternoon off by Gabe to attend the party, he had taken full advantage of the open bar and drunk rather more Champagne than he was accustomed to in the middle of the day.

Gabe gave him a withering look. "Oh, shut up Vincent. I'll say what I like. He's got nothing on me. And by the way, you look ridiculous."

Nathan looked at the solicitor and bit the inside of his cheeks to stop himself from grinning. Vincent Ramone was wearing Ava's floppy sun hat and looking just about as far removed from a hotshot solicitor as it was possible to look.

"Right. I'll continue." He cleared his throat. "We knew that Blake Hamilton had been poisoned. As was reported on the news, that was established very early in our investigation. What was more difficult to establish, though, was *why* he'd been poisoned, and *why* he was on your boat in the first place. Nothing was

Tapas, Carrot Cake and a Corpse

stolen, nothing was even disturbed. And the question also remained—how did he get on it?"

"I *told* you how he got on the boat." Gabe didn't bother to conceal his irritation. "I told you I must have left the gangplank unsecure when I went to the gym, making it easy for him to get on board and rob us."

"Hmmm. No, I don't think so, Mr. Driscoll. You see, I believe you were *expecting* Mr. Hamilton. I believe you were on the boat when he boarded it, at your invitation, after which you gave him a drink laced with your wife's medication before injecting him with weed killer."

There were horrified gasps around the table, the loudest from Samantha Driscoll who covered her face with her hands.

"Callously leaving Mr. Hamilton to die, you made your escape on the spare life boat, before destroying it and casting it back into the sea." Nathan leaned back in his chair. "Of course, you expected it to be taken out with the tide, which it was but, unfortunately for you, the tide also washed it up close to shore after the storm.

"Then you went to the gym and took a shower to clean yourself up, making a point of speaking to the receptionist on the way out to ensure he'd remember you'd been there."

Nathan reached down and took a large evidence bag out of the box he'd been carrying. Inside it were the remains of the life boat Garrett had found.

Gabe stared at him, his eyes moving from the evidence bag to Nathan's face. Suddenly, he threw his head back and laughed, slapping his thigh. "Oh, that's a good one Detective Chief Inspector! What a vivid imagination you must have. There's only one thing I have to say in response to your fantastic supposition." He stopped laughing and fixed Nathan with a stony glare. "Prove it."

Nathan returned the glare with a pleasant smile. "Oh, don't worry, Mr. Driscoll—

I'm getting there." He put the evidence bag back into the box and pulled out another one.

Gabe sat up straight in his seat and leaned forward to see what was inside.

"This was found along with the remains of the life boat." Nathan held up the bag. "It's Mr. Hamilton's wallet. The fact that all his credit cards are still in there, along with over £350, indicates that whoever killed him didn't want his money. They obviously had another reason to want him dead. Now, inside the wallet is something that we thought was a business card—until yesterday when another piece of evidence came to light that proved our assumptions wrong." Nathan bent forward again and took another evidence bag from the box, holding it up for Gabe to see. Inside was Blake's silver pendant.

"Oh no, no, no, no! Where did you get that? I got rid of it. I threw it into the sea!"

Nathan was caught a little off-guard when Gabe remained motionless in his seat and Samantha jumped up, shouting wildly.

"Mishis. Driscoll, I'd also shtrongly 'vise you to, um, shay nothing," Vincent Ramone slurred from behind Ava's hat, the brim of which was now completely obscuring his face.

"Oh, shut *up*, Vincent!" Samantha shouted, before flopping back down in her seat.

"Mrs. Driscoll?" Nathan said, enquiringly. "Would you care to elaborate?"

Samantha looked at him, then at Gabe, and burst into tears. "Gabe, you didn't kill Blake, did you? Please tell me you didn't kill him." She grabbed her husband's hand as she begged him to tell her the truth.

"What are you talking about, woman?! Of course I didn't kill him." Gabe shook her hand away.

"In that case, Mr. Driscoll. How do you explain this?" Nathan delved into the box again and pulled out the final, and most incriminating, piece of evidence.

Inside the bag was a syringe, an empty muscle relaxant pills box, and a bottle of weed killer.

For the first time that afternoon Gabe looked uncomfortable, but he continued with his denial. "I've never seen any of that stuff before."

"So how do you explain the fact that everything in this bag is covered in your fingerprints?"

Gabe's eyes darted around the table. "Why? Why would I kill him? What reason would I have had to kill Blake Hamilton?" He spluttered to his guests. "Why would …"

"*Gabe!*" Samantha interrupted him. Her voice was trembling and her face tear-stained. "Tell them. Just tell them, will you. If you don't, I will. I can't carry on like this."

Gabe put his head in his hands and said nothing.

"Perhaps this will shed some light on why you were so keen to see Mr. Hamilton dead." Nathan held up the bag with the silver pendant inside. It was open, as it had been when Charlotte had given it to him, and the photograph inside was clearly visible. In it, Gabe and Blake stood side by side, smiling widely at the camera, their arms draped around each other. In the top right-hand corner of the picture was blue sky and green palm trees—a perfect match to the previously unidentifiable 'business card' that had been found in Blake's wallet.

"It wasn't your wife who Blake was here to see, was it, Mr. Driscoll? It was you."

There were more gasps from around the table, but still Gabe said nothing.

Samantha's quiet voice spoke up. "Yes, it was." She turned to her husband. "I've got to tell him, Gabe. I know how difficult it's been for us to keep this secret, and how much it's damaged our relationship, but how could you have killed Blake because of it? How *could* you?" She blew her nose, loudly. "It's true. Blake was here to see Gabe—because he was in love with him. They met years ago, when Gabe's first wife was still alive, and they'd kept in touch ever since. When I met Gabe I thought they were just friends but, after we married, I found letters they'd sent to each other.

"It was obvious they were much more than friends and that Gabe had only married me to put people off the scent. He was petrified of someone finding out about his secret lover, about the person he loved with all his heart and wanted to spend his life with. He was scared that his kids would disown him and that he'd be shunned by all the members at his snobby country club. Being married to me was the perfect decoy.

"Not that our marriage was a complete sham, though." Samantha sniffed and smiled weakly as she looked around the table. "I really do love him and we've had some fabulous times. In fact, we decided to try and make a real go of things a few months ago. That's why we're here. We were going to sail around the country for a year to get away from it all but, wherever we went, Blake found us. We think he must have been tracking Gabe's phone.

"Anyway, when I found out that Blake was here I had to do something about it, so I followed him to his hotel to ask him to leave us alone. He was so smug. He laughed in my face and told me that Gabe would never love me like he loved him. He kept taunting me with the pendant Gabe gave him. He showed me the picture inside it and said he'd never stop following us until he'd taken Gabe away from me. I was so angry, I ripped it from his neck and ran off with it. Don't look so surprised, I could outrun any of you any day. I ran down to the beach and threw it into the sea. I didn't think I'd ever see it again."

She paused and took a sip of water.

"You see, Blake never forgave Gabe for marrying me and he never forgave me for taking Gabe away from him." She turned back to her husband. "Why did you have to kill him? We could have worked things out. We could have made him understand that you didn't want to see him anymore."

Gabe lifted his head and looked at her in disbelief.

""Worked things out?" "Didn't want to see him anymore?" You *stupid* woman! The reason I killed Blake is because I *couldn't* be with him, not because I didn't *want* to be with him. Every time I saw him, but had to keep my distance, I felt like my heart had been torn out of my chest. I loved him so much, but I couldn't risk people finding out about him. It would have ruined my life." His laugh was bitter. "And all this time, you've believed that Blake found us because he'd been tracking my phone? Oh no, my dear Samantha. He found us because I was calling him, *telling* him where we were. I couldn't bear the thought of not seeing him for so long."

Gabe sighed heavily, struggling to keep control of his emotions. "So you'll understand why the hardest thing I've ever had to do was leave him on the boat to die alone. And do you know what?" He put his face close to his wife's. "I will hate you for that until the day I die. The only reason I didn't get rid of the weed killer and the syringe was because I was saving them for you." His face contorted horribly with a twisted smile. "I hid my feelings well, don't you think?"

Samantha burst into tears again and sobbed as Ava, Harriett and Betty rushed to coo round and comfort her like mother hens.

Gabe stood up and turned to face Nathan. He knew what was coming.

"Gabe Driscoll, I am arresting you on suspicion of the murder of Blake Hamilton." He snapped his handcuffs onto Gabe's wrists behind his back as he continued with the caution, throughout which, Gabe's eyes focused on the ground.

As Nathan escorted him to the police car, Gabe raised his head. "Humour me for a moment, will you? Tell me, what led you to find the evidence I'd hidden?"

"Well, that, Mr. Driscoll," said Nathan, "is a very good question. You see, when you came back to the boat on the morning of the murder, the nails on one of your hands were dirty. Not unusual for some men but, on your perfectly-manicured hands, they stuck out a mile. In itself that wasn't enough to lead us to you, but when you struck up such a close friendship with Tom, that got us thinking. After that, it was only a matter of time before everything fell into place. Tom's hanging baskets were the perfect place to hide any incriminating evidence, explaining the dirt under your fingernails and, in befriending Tom, you gave yourself the perfect excuse to access them without arousing suspicion. A very clever hiding place, if I may say so. Whoever would have thought of looking on Tom's property for concealed evidence?

"If you'd only gone to the trouble of cleaning your nails after you'd hidden the bag, you could have got away, quite literally, with murder. Remember, it's often the smallest details that leave the biggest clues."

He caught Charlotte's eye and winked.

Chapter 13

"So anyway, are you free for dinner sometime next week? I know you have to work it around your shifts but any day is okay with me." Charlotte held the phone between her shoulder and her ear.

"Sounds good. How about Friday night? I'm not working, and you're not working the next day, so we can be grown-ups and stay out late."

"Actually, I…er…I meant dinner at my place. I'll cook." *Why do I feel so flustered? I've cooked dinner for Nathan a hundred times.*

"Oh, okay. That sounds even better. I'll bring the wine and beer. Listen, gotta go. Speak to you soon. Thanks for the invite."

Charlotte hung up, let out the breath she hadn't realised she'd been holding, and smiled.

oooooo

"That was the best meal I've had in a very long time. Thank you." Nathan put his cutlery down on his plate and sat back in his chair, his gaze fixed on Charlotte.

"Shall we take the wine and go and sit outside? It's so warm." She was starting to feel flustered again, as she had every time he'd looked at her that evening for longer than five seconds.

"Okay. I'll bring the bottle." Nathan followed close behind and pulled out one of the garden chairs for her to sit on.

"Thanks." She took the bottle from him and topped up her glass. *Oh boy, I'm going to need this.* She took a big gulp.

She was about to launch into her prepared speech, when Nathan said, "Is everything okay?"

It threw her a little off-course. "Er, yes, of course. Why shouldn't it be?"

"Well, it's like you've been trying to say something all evening, but then decide not to." Nathan looked at her, quizzically. "*Have* you been trying to say something?"

"Oh. Um, yes I have, actually." Based on the heat rising from her neck up, Charlotte deduced that her face must resemble an over-ripe tomato. Not really the look she'd been hoping for. "Oh damn it! Look, Nathan, I'm just going to say it and hope it doesn't ruin our friendship, okay? Please don't interrupt me, because it's going to be really hard for me to say this."

She took a deep breath.

"When I found out you weren't going out with Lucy Sanderson, I was *really* pleased. Happy, in fact." She stole a glance at him and saw that he was staring at her with an amused look on his face. She cleared her throat, and carried on. "So, anyway, um, I was really pleased that you weren't going out with *her* because I thought it might be nice if you were going out with *me* instead."

Oh no. That didn't come out at all like I'd planned it. Why on earth did I ever think this was a good idea?

"And now I'm so embarrassed, I can't even look at you," she said, miserably, and stood up to turn away from him.

Nathan put his glass down and went to stand behind her. He pulled her round gently to face him but she avoided his gaze, convinced it would be full of pity. Pity, because she wanted something with him that he would never want with her.

He's going to try and let me down gently, I know he is.

"Charlotte, will you look at me." He gently pulled her chin up with his finger. "I can't talk to you about this unless you look at me."

She looked at him and saw that his face was serious now.

"Charlotte, you shouldn't have said that."

Great. My humiliation is complete. I've really messed things up between us now.

Nathan continued. "*You* shouldn't have said it, because *I* should have said it. I should have said it ages ago. God knows, I've wanted to but I haven't had the guts. I couldn't bear to think that if I told you how I felt, it would ruin our friendship because you wouldn't feel the same."

What? Charlotte's mouth dropped open as the realization of what Nathan was telling her sunk in.

She began to smile.

She began to laugh.

"You're not just saying that to make me happy?" She grabbed his hands.

"Well, I *hope* it makes you happy but, no, I'm not *just* saying it because of that." He grinned.

She flung her arms around him and buried her face in the crook of his neck. She never wanted to let go.

He gently pushed her away from him to kiss her softly and she felt fireworks go off in her chest. It had been so long since anyone had kissed her she thought her knees were going to give way.

When they came up for air she took his hand. "Shall we go inside?"

"I hope you're not going to corrupt me?" He fixed her with a stern look. "I *am* an officer of the law, you know."

"Well, if I do… you'll just have to put me in handcuffs." Charlotte squealed with laughter as he chased her into the house.

CHAPTER 14

On the day that would have been Charlotte's parents' 40th wedding anniversary, a fishing boat left the marina just before dusk.

On board were Garrett, Laura, Jess, Ava, Harriett, Betty, Tom, Nathan, and Charlotte.

After all that had happened, Charlotte realised that she didn't want to keep her parents' ashes at home any more. She wanted them to be scattered out at sea, for them to be free to drift, mingle and whirl with the tide, not be confined to ceramic urns.

Her life was taking a new direction now. With Nathan, she was happier than she'd been in years. She hadn't realised how much she'd wanted someone in her life to love, and to love her, and she couldn't have wished for a better partner than the man who was standing at her side.

As for the others, they were like family. *True* family. Not a family you had but never spoke to, but a real, loving, strong family. She loved every single one of them with all her heart.

As the sun began to set, Garrett dropped anchor and the boat came to a stop, bobbing gently on the calm sea. The air was still and, except for the lapping of the water against the hull, there wasn't a sound to be heard.

"Are you ready?"

Charlotte had been ready for this ever since she'd first talked to Garrett about it two months ago but now it was time, she wasn't so sure.

"I don't know…" She gulped down the lump that rose in her throat. She didn't want to cry. She wanted this to be a joyful occasion.

Nathan put his arms around her and she snuggled into his chest. "You don't have to do this, you know," he whispered. "No one will care if we just turn the boat around and go back home."

"*I'll* care. No, no, I want to do it." She pulled away from him and lifted one of the ceramic urns from the deck. Closing her eyes, she removed its lid and offered up a few silent words of prayer before upturning the urn and emptying the contents into the sea. Then she did the same with the other one.

She gulped again and squeezed her eyes tight shut. *Don't cry, don't cry.*

Garrett stepped forward and recited a short blessing. As he spoke, his gruff voice cracked on the last line of the verse.

"Molly and Scott,

May your spirits soar high and free,

May your love be ever present,

May we keep you always in our hearts,

And may God keep you close in His kingdom.

God bless you both."

He hugged Charlotte before stepping back and blinking hard. Like her, he hadn't realised how emotional this moment would be.

"Here." Nathan was holding the box of lilies Charlotte had collected from the florist that morning. "Take one."

She took a flower and tossed it onto the water and everyone followed suit before crowding round and enveloping her in a huge, loving, group hug. The tears fell freely now and she didn't try to stop them. Taking a deep breath, she let it out slowly and felt all her tension melt away.

As the sun began to dip below the horizon, Charlotte watched the flowers bobbing on the barely rippling surface of the sea. "I love you forever, Mum and Dad," she whispered. "Sleep tight, both of you."

As she watched the light fade, she couldn't think of a more perfect way to end that chapter of her life and, as Nathan planted a gentle kiss on her lips, a better way to begin the next.

Turning to her friends she smiled and said, "Let's go home."

The End

Please visit my website at sherribryan.com to sign up to my readers' list if you'd like to receive a notification when further releases in The Charlotte Denver Cozy Mystery Series are published.

Each book contains a new mystery to solve, and is a stand-alone story, so they can be read in any order but, if you'd like to read them as they were written after this book, this is the order to follow;
Fudge Cake, Felony and a Funeral – Book Two
Spare Ribs, Secrets and a Scandal – Book Three

Pumpkins, Peril and a Paella – Book Four

Hamburgers, Homicide and a Honeymoon – Book Five

Crab Cakes, Killers and a Kaftan – Book Six

Mince Pies, Mistletoe and Murder - Book Seven

A SELECTION OF RECIPES FROM TAPAS, CARROT CAKE AND A CORPSE

SWEET CHILLI PRAWNS

Serves 4 as tapas or 2 as a light lunch

INGREDIENTS

- 8 large raw prawns. Shelled and de—veined, but with the tail left on
- 3 tablespoons olive oil
- Chopped flat leaf parsley, to serve

FOR THE SAUCE

- 3 tablespoons tomato ketchup
- 1 tablespoon caster sugar
- 1 teaspoon white wine **or** apple cider vinegar
- 1 smallish, fresh red chilli, finely chopped **or** ½ teaspoon chilli flakes

- 2 or 3 large garlic cloves (depending on how much you like garlic!) peeled and crushed

<u>METHOD</u>

1. Mix all the sauce ingredients together in a bowl and put to one side.
2. Heat the olive oil in a large frying pan over a medium heat and add the prawns. Cook until they are pink throughout, turning once — how long this takes will depend on the size of the prawns.
3. About a minute before the prawns have finished cooking, add the sauce to the pan and cook everything together for the last minute.
4. Tip into a serving dish and sprinkle with fresh, flat leaf parsley.
5. Serve with crusty bread

BUFFALO WING AND CHICKPEA STEW

INGREDIENTS

- 1lb buffalo chicken wings, with the drumette attached
- 1 onion, finely chopped
- 1 garlic clove, crushed
- 2 carrots, finely chopped
- 1 tablespoon sweet paprika
- 8 oz smoked bacon, chopped
- 14oz can chickpeas (garbanzos), rinsed and drained
- 14oz can crushed tomatoes
- 4 fl oz rosé wine (You can use white if you prefer, or replace it with stock)
- 7fl oz chicken stock
- 2 tbsp olive oil
- Salt and pepper to taste
- A handful of chopped fresh parsley

METHOD

1. In a large pan, heat 1 tablespoon of the oil over a medium heat.
2. Add the chicken to the pan and fry, turning a few times, until golden brown. (This step is not to cook the chicken completely — that comes later — so at this stage, just make sure it's nice and brown).
3. Remove the chicken from the pan and cover it with tinfoil to keep warm.
4. Add the remaining oil to the pan, along with the onion, carrot, garlic and bacon and cook over a gentle heat for five minutes, or until the onion and carrot are soft and the bacon is well browned.
5. Spoon or drain most of the fat from the pan (leave about a teaspoon behind) and add the paprika. Cook for a minute and then add the wine (or stock if you prefer) and simmer until it has reduced by half.

Tapas, Carrot Cake and a Corpse

6. Add the crushed tomatoes, stock, chickpeas and salt and pepper to the pan, and bring everything to a boil.
7. Return the chicken to the pan and turn the heat down to a simmer. Cover the pan with a lid and cook until the chicken is completely cooked through. This should take about 25 to 30 minutes but, depending on the size of the chicken pieces, could take a little less or more time to cook.
8. Check the dish for seasoning, scatter with the fresh parsley and serve.

TORTILLA DE PATATAS (Potato Omelette)

INGREDIENTS

- 2 lbs of potatoes, peeled and thinly sliced
- 2 large onions, peeled and thinly sliced (You can leave these out if you prefer — many people in Spain don't use anything other than potatoes, oil, eggs and salt in their tortilla, but I like the flavour of the onion.)
- 8 large eggs, whisked
- 1 teaspoon fresh thyme **or** ½ teaspoon dried thyme (Again, you can leave this out if you prefer. Personally, I love it!)
- ½ cup of olive oil (I know this sounds like a lot of oil, but it doesn't make the tortilla greasy, and it makes a big difference to the end result. I've tried it with less oil, and it doesn't taste nearly as good. If you don't want to use that much oil, this recipe will still work with less — it just won't taste quite the same.)

- Salt and Pepper to taste

METHOD

1. Put the oil into a 10" non-stick frying pan over a medium heat.
2. Add the sliced potatoes to the pan and cook over a medium heat for five minutes, or until they begin to soften.
3. Add the sliced onions and thyme (if using) to the potatoes, with salt and pepper to taste, and cook for a further five minutes, stirring everything together well.
4. Add the beaten eggs to the pan and with a wooden spoon or plastic spatula, mix them quickly into the potato mixture until everything is well combined.
5. Turn the heat down to low and shake the pan to prevent the omelette from catching on the bottom.
6. Leave to cook gently until the eggs are set.

7. **If you have a grill and a pan with a heatproof handle**, put it under a medium heat for a minute or two to brown the top of the omelette a little. **If you don't have a grill**, when the omelette is cooked, carefully hold a lid over the pan using a cloth and pour off any excess oil. Be careful not to burn yourself or to let the omelette tip out. Then, put a large plate over the pan and quickly flip it over. Then slide the omelette back into the pan to sit over a medium heat for a minute or two to brown the top, which is now the bottom. **NOTE:** You can leave out this step if you want to. The omelette will still be cooked, just a little pale. If you are going to do it though, again, take care not to burn yourself. I'd recommend that you hold the pan handle and the plate with a cloth and do it over a sink or the kitchen worktop.

8. Turn off the heat and allow the omelette to cool in the pan, before turning it out, cutting into wedges and serving.

NOTE: This omelette is best eaten lukewarm, but it's good cold too. It also makes a delicious sandwich filling or brunch dish, served with crispy bacon and grilled tomatoes.

Sherri Bryan

BAKED WHITING FILLETS WITH CHERRY TOMATOES, TARRAGON AND CAPERS

INGREDIENTS

- 2 Whiting fillets
- A little oil
- A small glass dry white wine
- 2 teaspoons fresh tarragon leaves
- 2 cloves garlic, broken open with a rolling pin or flat knife blade
- 1 lemon
- 2 teaspoons capers
- 10 whole cherry tomatoes
- Salt and pepper to taste

METHOD

1. Preheat the oven to 180°C.
2. You will need two sheets of baking paper (you can use tinfoil if you don't have baking paper), big enough to make a parcel around the fish, leaving a space at the top.

3. Brush a little oil onto the sheet to help prevent the fish from sticking.
4. Place a slice of lemon in the centre of the sheet. Place the fish fillet on top and put five whole cherry tomatoes, a teaspoon of capers and a garlic clove around it.
5. Season well with salt and pepper and then scatter a teaspoon of tarragon leaves on top of the fish.
6. Bring up the sides of the sheet and add half a glass of wine to each parcel, together with a squeeze of lemon juice.
7. Seal the parcel. **NOTE:** Don't forget to leave a space at the top of the parcel so the fish has room to steam.
8. Bake in the preheated oven for 12 to 15 minutes.
9. Open the parcels at the table, taking care to keep your hands away from the steam that will billow out. The smell is gorgeous and the taste is even better!

NOTE: These are good served with steamed green beans or wilted spinach, buttered carrots and baby potatoes.

CARROT CAKE

Serves 10

INGREDIENTS

FOR THE CAKE

- **10 oz plain flour**
- **2 level teaspoons baking powder**
- **1 level teaspoon bicarbonate of soda**
- **1 level teaspoon salt**
- **2 level teaspoons ground cinnamon**
- **1 level teaspoon ground ginger**
- **1 level teaspoon ground nutmeg**
- 7 oz dark brown sugar
- 3½ oz caster sugar
- 4 large beaten eggs
- 9 fl oz sunflower oil (or half sunflower oil, half olive oil)
- 1 tablespoon vanilla extract
- 4 carrots, peeled and grated (about 1 lb in weight)

- 14 oz can crushed pineapple, well drained
- 4 oz pecans, chopped (if you don't want to put these in, substitute with one extra carrot)

FOR THE ICING

- 6 oz softened cream cheese (leave out of the fridge for a while)
- 2 oz softened, unsalted butter
- 1 teaspoon vanilla extract
- 9 oz icing (powdered) sugar
- 1 to 2 tablespoons milk

METHOD

1. Preheat oven to 180ºC/350ºF/Gas mark 4. Line a 13" x 9" tin with non-stick baking paper.
2. Sift the first seven ingredients **only** into a large bowl, and then stir in the sugars until blended together. Make a well in the centre.
3. In a jug or bowl, beat together the eggs, oil and vanilla extract and pour the mixture into the well. Using an electric beater on a slow speed, gradually draw the flour mixture from the side of the bowl and then turn up the speed and beat until a smooth batter forms.
4. Stir in the carrots and the crushed pineapple (and chopped nuts if using) until everything is mixed together well.
5. Pour the mixture into the prepared tin and smooth the surface with the back of a spoon or a pallet knife.

6. Bake in the centre of the preheated oven for 50 minutes to one hour, or until the cake is firm and a skewer inserted into the middle comes out clean. (In my oven, it normally takes about an hour and 15 minutes to cook.)
7. Remove the cake from the oven and leave to completely cool before removing from the tin and discarding the baking paper.
8. Make the icing by beating together the cream cheese, softened butter and vanilla extract until smooth, and then gradually beating in the icing sugar until it's all combined. Add a little milk if necessary to help make the icing a spreadable consistency and then decorate the top of the cake with it.
9. Refrigerate for about an hour before cutting into squares and serving.

Tapas, Carrot Cake and a Corpse

NOTE: I've made this cake before just with granulated sugar when I haven't had brown or caster sugar, and it's turned out fine. I've also used mixed spice when I haven't had any ginger and it was okay, and I've also made it without nuts. Again, it was perfectly fine.

A NOTE FROM SHERRI

Hello, and thanks so much for reading my first Cozy Mystery novella, *Tapas, Carrot Cake and a Corpse.*

Set in the fictional UK town of St. Eves, the location was inspired by many happy holidays spent in the beautiful English counties of Cornwall and Devon, and by Spain, the country I now call home.

It was a joy to write, and I really hope you enjoyed it. If you did, I would love to hear from you. Your feedback is very important to me—constructive criticism included! Also, if you'd like to, I'd really appreciate it if you'd consider leaving me a review on Amazon.

I should mention that although this book has been proofread and edited more times than I can recall, there may still be the odd mistake within its pages. If you should come across one, I'd be grateful if you could let me know so I can put it right.

You can contact me by email at sherri@sherribryan.com, on Twitter @sbryanauthor or on Facebook at https://www.facebook.com/sherribryanauthor.

Even if you'd just like to say 'hi', just drop me a message and introduce yourself—I'd love for you to get in touch!

Anyway, if you'd like to receive notifications for forthcoming books, along with details of free downloads from time to time, please visit my website at sherribryan.com or my Facebook page, where you can sign up to my mailing list. Please don't worry, I respect your privacy and I promise I won't flood your inbox with messages, nor will I ever share your name or email address with anyone!

Thanks again for taking an interest in my book. I hope you'll enjoy the rest of The Charlotte Denver Cozy Mystery series.

Wishing you warm regards,
Sherri Bryan.

ABOUT SHERRI BRYAN

Sherri read her first cozy mystery in 2014 and her love of the genre began that day.

Having read many more, she decided to write her own and her debut book, Tapas, Carrot Cake and a Corpse, was published in May 2015.

Apart from writing, her main interests include her rescue dog, cooking, reading eating out and watching crime dramas. When she's not tapping away at her keyboard, you'll find her playing with her dog, experimenting with ingredients in the kitchen, curled up with a book or dreaming up new cozy mystery plots.

Tapas, Carrot Cake and a Corpse, the first in the Charlotte Denver Cozy Mystery Series, was followed by *Fudge Cake, Felony and a Funeral*, *Spare Ribs, Secrets and a Scandal, Pumpkins, Peril and a Paella, Hamburgers, Homicide and a Honeymoon,*

Crab Cakes, Killers and a Kaftan and *Mince Pies, Mistletoe and Murder.*

She is currently working on the eighth book in the Charlotte Denver series, as well as a new cozy mystery series.

Sherri Bryan

ALL RIGHTS RESERVED

No part of this publication may be reproduced, distributed, or transmitted in any form, or by any means, including photocopying, recording, or other electronic or mechanical methods, without the prior written permission of the copyright owner, and publisher, of this piece of work, except in the case of brief quotations embodied in critical reviews

This is a work of fiction. All names, characters, businesses, organizations, places, events and incidents are either the products of the author's imagination, or are used in an entirely fictitious manner.

Any other resemblance to organizations, actual events or actual persons, living or dead, is purely coincidental.

Published by Sherri Bryan Copyright ©2015

Printed in Poland
by Amazon Fulfillment
Poland Sp. z o.o., Wrocław